BBC NATIONAL SHORT STORY AWARD 2022

BBC

National
Short Story
Award 2022

with Cambridge University

First published in Great Britain in 2022 by Comma Press.
www.commapress.co.uk

'Flat 19' by Jenn Ashworth first published in *Close to Midnight*
(Flame Tree Press, 2022). 'Green Afternoon' by Vanessa
Onwuemezi first published in 6*Dark Neighbourhood*
(Fitzcarraldo Editions, 2021). 'Blue 4eva' by Saba Sams first
published in *Send Nudes* (Bloomsbury, 2022).

A CIP catalogue record of this book is available
from the British Library.

ISBN-10: 1-912697-64-5
ISBN-13: 978-1-91269-764-9

The publisher gratefully acknowledges the support
of Arts Council England.

Supported using public funding by

**ARTS COUNCIL
ENGLAND**

Printed and bound in the US by IPG.

MIX
Paper | Supporting
responsible forestry
FSC® C013604

Contents

Introduction

IN MANY RESPECTS, I am underqualified for the job of writing this introduction. I have never won or even been shortlisted for a short story prize myself. In fact, I remember entering my first as an enthusiastic seventeen-year-old. The competition in question was run by a local writers' circle in Malvern, where I went to school. I poured my heart and soul into my story, which ran to several typed pages and contained sentences of great earnestness as I attempted to relay the entire life of a married couple, from their meeting at university to the tragic early death of the wife from cancer. The judges were kind to me, and said they'd enjoyed reading my submission but that it felt more like a synopsis for a novel than a short story.

It was a perspicacious observation and it stayed with me. In the years that followed, I wrote a few more short stories and tried to get better but I spent more of my time reading the work of others. As I made my way through the collections of Katherine Mansfield, Raymond Carver, Helen Simpson, Jon McGregor, George Saunders, Alice Monroe, Lydia Davis, Chimamanda Ngozi Adichie, Jhumpa Lahiri and many more, I could see quite clearly what those judges had meant. When, in our early 30s, a friend and I set up a live initiative called Pin Drop which involved authors and actors reading short stories in beautiful settings, I understood even more deeply that the success of a short story relies not only on the read sentences, but on the ones that have been edited out.

As ever with this competition, there was a notable omission from the start of the judging process. My fellow judges and I read the stories without knowing the author's name – a crucial element of our decision-making, which meant none of us was swayed by anyone's professional reputation or lack of it. When it came to deciding our shortlist there was a great deal of common ground between us despite our varied professional and personal backgrounds. We were impressed by the high quality and struck by some recurring themes.

This was a year which saw a lot of writers trying to make sense of the pandemic – Covid made an appearance in several stories, while other entrants transposed our lived experience to invented apocalyptic scenarios. There were quite a few stories which featured clones and artificial intelligence, and I for one was convinced that Kazuo Ishiguro must have entered several times over as so much of the prose seemed close in tone to his bestselling novel, *Klara and the Sun* (I mean this as a compliment). The idea of outsidership cropped up repeatedly and some of the most moving stories concerned themselves with the concept of not belonging; of being cast adrift by a society shaped by a wilful misunderstanding of otherness.

But although so many of these short stories were good, only a few of them were great. A good short story says something meaningful. A great short story keeps certain things hidden. The best short stories find their power on the page precisely because of what the author has decided not to say. The space around the words gives sense to the words themselves, in the same way as a striking piece of sculpture makes us look not only at the object itself but at how it changes its surroundings.

When we reach the final sentence of a great short story, we should feel that the world imagined by the writer is so coherent, so encompassing that it exists both within and beyond the page. We do not need to know everything about this imaginative world, but we need to have confidence that the author does. Above all, reading a short story should be a satisfying experience in and of itself. To do all this, while resisting the temptation to write too much, is a real talent.

The five stories in this anthology are fine examples of this talent. Their subject matters are varied – step-families, road trips through America, AI clones, a post-apocalyptic love affair, and urban knife crime – but they are connected by a surety of touch. Every one of these writers has taken great care to choose the shining details that arrest our attention, to inflect their paragraphs with precision and unique lyrical flair without ever losing grip on the pace or purpose of the story in question.

In 'Blue4Eva', Saba Sams lures the reader in

with a sun-soaked holiday setting, before sowing the seeds of an altogether more discomfiting atmosphere lurking beneath the blue surface of the swimming pool. It is an authentic portrayal of the often tense dynamics of blended familial relationships, with a truthfulness to the dialogue that impressed us all. We were particularly enamoured by Sams's portrayal of twelve-year-old Stella whose likeable warmth and strength of character was more than equal to the creepy power of her voyeuristic stepfather, whose attachment to his new, expensive camera prompted us to ask questions about the male gaze and ownership.

Anna Bailey's 'Long Way to Come for a Sip of Water' is a gorgeously written evocation of modern America. In this story of repression and emotional damage, the disputed inheritance of a family home mirrors the broader issue of who is given the right to exist authentically in a country still at war with itself. Individual sentences were written with deftness and beauty, and the exploration of sexual identity was sensitively done.

This was also the case in 'And the moon descends on the temple that was' by Kerry

Andrew. Of all the post-apocalyptic stories we read this year, the judges felt that Andrew's story spoke of a real human compassion that made it stand apart from the others. The use of imagery in the story was praised, as was Andrew's ability to write sexually fluid characters without judgment or prurience. It felt as though there was a beating heart underpinning each carefully judged paragraph. Although much of the story concerns itself with the ever-present shadow of a deathly virus, the vividness of the characters ensured there was still life to the prose.

While Andrew's story concerned itself with a dystopian future, Vanessa Onwuemezi's 'Green Afternoon' opens with a boy dying of a stab wound in the arms of a narrator in the present day. Out of all the shortlisted stories, this was the one that the judges felt most benefitted from re-visiting. The evocative richness of the prose demands our sustained attention, and every new reading reveals some integral detail we might previously have missed. The freshness of Onwuemezi's narrative voice, combined with her Joycean prose style and her rhythmic, captivating command of language left us all breathless.

As you might have gathered, there wasn't an enormous amount of humour on display in this year's submissions. But 'Flat 19' by Jenn Ashworth did contain welcome flashes of laughter in its skewering of middle-class pretension and the sometimes stultifying demands of a long marriage. Our narrator is a successful artist, but also a put-upon mother, wife and daughter, who finds her own identity flattened by her efforts to meet everyone else's needs. She hits upon an unexpected and ingenious solution (spoiler alert: it involves clones). The strength of Ashworth's writing distinguished this particular clone story from many of the others, as did its readability and ability to engage from the first sentence. The ending lodged in my mind for weeks after I finished reading – a perfect example of leaving a story at a point of interest, rather than tying everything up too neatly.

These stories represent the new vanguard of British writing. My judges and I were pleasantly surprised, when the names of the authors were revealed, to find that only one of them (Kerry Andrew) had made the shortlist before. Although many of 2022's entries imagined post-apocalyptic dystopias, perhaps in response to our current troubled times, I am confident that the short story, at least, is in safe hands. The writers in this anthology will ensure its future is bright for many years to come.

Elizabeth Day
London, 2022

And the moon descends on the temple that was

Kerry Andrew

THE NEXT TOWN IS the same.

Leaves in the drains, making a lake of the road, water furling beyond his wheels. No flags. The smell bad, even from inside the truck.

He collects what he needs, moves on.

He turns off at a sign with butterflies framing an indigenous name. The buildings on the main street are cream-coloured – antique store, barber's, home improvement place with the grille down. The sign on the bank says *TEMPORARILY CLOSED.* There's still meat in the butcher's window, though it's unrecognisable. A bus parked on the corner with one low tyre. Round the corner, he starts seeing the flags.

He cruises round the edge of town. Prefers a small place, houses far apart, no flags. A garage for the pick-up. Outside a one-level condo, the realtor sign is stuck in the long grass – a smiling white woman in a blouse with her arms folded.

It's as he hoped. The rooms bare, TV cable hanging loose. Dust sits thick on the counters, and the cupboards are empty. No beds, so he gets his ground mat and pillow. Makes sure all the curtains are shut.

★

He thinks he's imagining it at first, phantoms in his ears.

He lies on his back, hands folded over his sleeping bag. Listens. Liquid shapes in the air. A melody and falling handfuls of sound. He pulls on his clothes.

Outside, the clouds are moving fast. He sees the street afresh with this new sound, the emptiness painted with light. Space.

He follows the strange, shimmering music down the street, round the corner to a big old clapboard house, lemon-yellow and grand for

2

this town, windows open. No flags around.

He walks round the house. The music stops, repeats.

The side door is ajar.

Inside, there's no smell. The music is coming from a triangle of daylight at the end of the hallway, which is long and dark, photos of a guy in an army uniform, a woman with two kids and a Dalmatian.

He gets to the doorway, rolls his head around the frame.

In a wood-panelled room, a young man is at a grand piano. He looks down at his hands as they move. The lid of the piano is held up by its stick.

He's eighteen or so. Olive-skinned, in a pale pink T-shirt.

The piano sings from right inside itself. Each note sends ripples out into the room. The music has suspended each of his cells, winnows to nothing but a single line.

He shifts and the floorboard creaks. The pianist looks up and stops playing, as if a sentence has been cut off.

You alone?

The pianist nods. There's nothing but a sense of that broken piano note still hanging in the air, dividing into dust motes.

Do you have it?

No.

Sure about that?

Do you?

He doesn't answer, begins to step back into the darkness of the hallway.

Wait. You want breakfast?

The kitchen has a blackened brick fireplace, an old-style oven. Cans, pulses. The sink's a mess.

They eat beans, artichokes and tuna at an oak table that jerks every time the pianist leans over his plate. His eyes keep dashing over to him.

This your house?

No.

Your town?

The pianist shakes his head, runs a nail over his lip, which is dry, serrated. *From upstate.* The table jerks. *You?*

East, he says. *Anyone else here?*

I'm the last.

As he finishes his final mouthful, he stands.

Nods. *May wellness be within you*, people would say.

Alright, he says. Turns, doesn't look back.

Hey. The pianist has followed him to the front stoop, fingers drumming his thigh, tapping the rail. He's rangy, an inch or so taller. *Can I come with you?*

I travel alone.

Did you have other options?

He heads down the front yard path.

When did you last see someone else like you?

He can't remember.

Please, the pianist says, a catch in his voice.

He keeps walking.

He packs up his sleeping gear. Metal bowl and gas stove. Drives to the end of the road, sits there for a long time, turns back towards the yellow house.

The pianist is sitting on the stoop, elbows on knees, head hanging down.

He stops by the fence, turns off the ignition.

The pianist lifts his head.

The pianist talks as if he hasn't in a long while. After a time, he stops suddenly, rests his temple against the glass. Watches the tall cornfields.

Listen, he says, looking over from the driver's seat. *If we're going to do this, there need to be rules.*

OK.

Less talking.

OK.

If I want you to leave, you leave.

OK.

I don't want to know about you, or your past. Nothing like that.

The pianist looks out of the window. Back. *Gonna tell me your name at least?*

He remembers the last time he gave it, how it was called over and over from different rooms, then just one room. Worn out until he didn't have any attachment to it at all.

He looks at the cracked asphalt in front of him. *Ben.*

I'm Joshua.

★

A container yard. A kestrel on the telephone wire. Low fog on the fields.

They take quiet roads. You wouldn't know any different, except for the crops and the occasional car having drifted off into the ditch.

Joshua's presence, though he's stopped talking, is intrusive, shocking. He's nineteen, though seems younger. There's a restlessness in him, middle finger tapping on his knee, arm hanging out of the window. Singing under his breath, just enough to be heard, not enough to know what he's singing. He rifles in the bag he quickly packed, offers potato chips.

Ben shakes his head.

They pass a grain silo, a monolith with a curved silver roof. A canvas sign droops over its dome, the words roughly painted: *PRAY*

Do you have any music? Joshua says.

Sorry.

He's aware that Joshua is looking at the beads hanging from the rearview mirror, behind him at the tarp covering the back. He plucks a short, coarse hair from his seat. *Did you have a dog?* he asks.

It wasn't my truck.

He watches the sky, its colour and temperament, though it's nothing but vast, blue.

Joshua puts his feet up on the dash.

Ben glances over, looks again, and veers over to the side of the road, hitting the brakes. Joshua slams his shoulder into the door.

You said you didn't have it.

I don't.

What the fuck is that? He gestures to where Joshua's jeans have ridden up. The circular red welt, slightly raised, above his ankle bone.

It's not what you think.

Out.

I did it to myself.

Ben looks at him.

I heated a metal bottle and burnt myself. Joshua pulls up the leg of his jeans. Two more faint welts, exactly the same size.

Why?

Why d'you think?

Ben puts his elbow on the window ledge, stares outwards, thumb knuckle against his mouth.

I'm not lying.

Come here.

Joshua leans over, and Ben uses his forefinger to pull down the skin of Joshua's under-eye, carefully lifts his eyelid. Does the same to the other. His irises are as blue as cornflowers.

Tongue.

Joshua sticks out his tongue for a moment,

and curls it up. A sweet, stale smell.

They sit back.

Ben stares at the road. *OK*, he says.

★

As evening comes in, they reach a town with a tall water tower and a fire station. The flagged houses are around the central crux of streets, near the grocery and convenience store. The first place with a realtor's sign is still occupied. The second is better – sage-green walls, recent floorboards. Marble effect tiles in the bathroom.

Joshua has wandered through, returned to the living room. *Don't you want one with… stuff?* he asks.

Nope.

He beats a rhythm on the doorframe as he watches Ben dump his sleeping bag and ground mat down. *I kinda need a bed.*

Ben doesn't look up. *Sleep where you want. I don't care.* He's aware of Joshua hovering for a moment longer before he disappears.

Ben listens to the night-whispers of the house. Feels the presence of Joshua somewhere in the town, wonders whether he'll come back. His stomach grumbles. He'd taken a few things from the store, couldn't be bothered to use his gas stove, eaten dry cereal from the box.

Maybe he'll stay a few nights. Being on the road makes his neck ache. Tonight had brought a new tiredness, the effort of having to *be* someone all day.

He's just drifting off when there's a new creak. In his half-sleep, he sits up and fumbles for a weapon that doesn't exist, hears the person come in. Tall, slender, carrying a cloud.

Joshua doesn't say anything. Doubles up one comforter at the opposite end of the room and lies down, brings the other one over him.

Ben doesn't sleep.

★

In the morning, Ben wakes to find a can of evaporated milk by his feet. A ceramic bowl and a spoon engraved with herringbone lines. Joshua's bedding is rolled up in the corner.

Ben stands on the lawn in his bare feet, the grass calf-high, the wildflowers huge. Eats his cereal. Watches the sky. A great-tailed grackle sails past, a brief glimmer of blue-black, joining others on a white oak. Their arid, shit-eating chuckle.

Then he hears it, and this time knows what it is. He swears, and goes back inside for his sneakers.

The sound has a way of pearling the air but he finds him, past a kindergarten and a place selling stained glass. The windows all open, front door wide.

Joshua is at an upright piano, his back to him. Playing something wild and thunderous, right foot hitting the pedal, hands overtaking each other.

Hey, Ben says. Repeats it, louder. Stalks over.

Joshua glances at him, keeps playing. He only stops when Ben takes his hand off the keys. *What?*

You trying to get us found?

There's no one here. He returns his right hand to its falling pattern, then puts a hand in his hair. *It's so out of tune.*

We gotta go. Ben tries not to sound panicked. The piano is as loud as a siren.

Joshua gazes at him abstractedly.

Now.

You got it. He stands, lifts up the red velvet lid of the piano stool, and flicks through the music books. Selects a couple, closes the lid.

★

What did you do? Before? Joshua asks.

Ben keeps driving. Bugs silt up the windshield.

Joshua doesn't press. Jiggles his knees.

Can you stop doing that?

I can't help it.

He doesn't mind, really. It means Joshua doesn't have it.

What's the capital of Malaysia?

What?

Gotta talk about something.

Ben draws in a deep breath.

Maybe that's too hard. Iran.

Can't you just look at the road? Count fences?

Come on. Just this one.

Kuala Lumpur. Tehran.

Capital of Uruguay.

A short pause. *Montevideo.*

Joshua takes in a thoughtful, amused breath between his teeth. *I underestimated you.*

Yeah, Ben says. *You did.*

★

Ben finds Joshua out in the back yard as dusk falls. He's watching the sunset over the fence, biting on his thumbnail.

Another anonymous house, linoleum and chrome, generic photo canvas art on the walls. No books. No plants. Joshua had brought in the comforters from last night's town, rolled them in the corner of the room where Ben had dumped his own bedding.

Ben eyes the sky. Cool pink rubbed over the top of muted grey clouds.

Want a drink of something? Joshua's voice sounds distant, emotionless. *I got liquor.*

Sure. I'll go.

Ben comes back out with two plain white mugs, pours them both a fingerful of bourbon.

The pink fattens into molten layers, digs itself into the clouds. The pink is almost neon. He's aware of Joshua's stillness next to his own, beyond fear.

Did you lose people? Joshua asks.

Mmm-hmm. That wasn't the question, of course. It needed to be preceded by *when*. He can't return it. He hasn't got the capacity for whatever the answer will be.

13

Slowly, the deep plum colours take over, as they should, the pink becoming an afterthought. The moon's a snipped crescent, high in the east.

Ben hears the air rise in Joshua's chest, hold for a long moment before releasing, short and heavy. He knows it's the breath that both of them have needed this whole time in the garden.

Joshua finally stops biting his nail.

They go back inside.

★

They stay another night. Joshua disappears for most of the day, saying he'll be careful. Ben does his rounds of reps, looks in on a couple of houses. Breaks into the places he can bear to.

He collects torches, candles, matches and lighters, finds a garage with cans of diesel. Looks over the pick-up. He fills the water canisters, takes a shower with what's left, the water briefly lukewarm, then cold, then gone. He checks his eyes, tongue. Eats some of the pickled gherkins Joshua got yesterday. Pretzels and peanuts. He fancies he hears a piano, far off.

Joshua comes back wearing aviator sunglasses and a checked pork pie hat. He has two books and an armful of CDs. *For the road.*

You don't mind the smell?

He shrugs. *Used to it*, he says, before pulling out some teenager's diary he's found, and reading it until the end.

★

They fall into a rhythm. Joshua never asks why they're taking a certain road, though sometimes points to a turning to see what's at the end. A wartime internment camp, a fort, a rock circle surrounded by a fence tied with hundreds of coloured cloths. They always find a place before dusk.

Joshua returns from his days wearing a different T-shirt, usually a band's logo, and Ben never sees the old one again. He produces a harmonica, a huge hardback atlas. Swaps his towels, colourful beach varieties and monogrammed washcloths. He paints his fingernails with dark grey nail polish. Blue eyeliner.

He plays DJ, tossing out the CDs he doesn't like. They listen to dance tracks, country duets, gospel, concertos.

They look out for fruit trees. Corn fields. Health food stores. Farms, if only for eggs.

They both watch the sky.

15

They come upon a place where prairie faces mountain, with its own gas and water supply, fire and log store. It's empty, but its owners are everywhere. A patchwork quilt with West African fabrics, anniversary cards, plants, crisped and leafless. An old upright piano.

Joshua plays it for hours every day, and Ben goes on long walks just to clear his head. But often, he sits out on the porch, tries to read something. Joshua plays jazz tunes, a couple that Ben faintly recognises, though Joshua seems to twist them, make them journey in unpredictable ways.

He often plays the piece that Ben walked in on. Explains about the type of scale the French composer used, how it's partly influenced by Javanese gamelan music, how the unresolved harmonies give the impression of no start or end point.

Ben hears new things in it every time. How a melody is shadowed, clung to. Notes near the bottom of the piano, right at the top, and wide space in between. Chords from beyond the sky.

★

Was it red where you were? Joshua asks.

It's raining, hard. Pools forming outside the door, the roof sounding penetrable.

Ben looks over, and back at his travel-size bottle of vermouth. *Kinda pink. I don't know.*

He did know. He'd woken up to a sky blazing the pink of deep wounds, thought it must only be sunrise, found it was noon. It hurt to look at, but he'd thought that the hangover talking. When making coffee he noticed the fine dust-grains on the window. Realised how many sirens he was hearing.

Did you have family?

Yeah.

It stayed for three days. The pink of the underside of things. Of amaranths. The strange smell, acrid and cordite.

A wife and daughter.

Daughter. Reduced to a word that spoke nothing of the little girl who hopped, rode her scooter into puddles, liked drawing mutant cactus plants and knew all the words to classic disco songs.

They were with you?

He shook his head.

Joshua doesn't say sorry, just smoothes his forefinger around the rim of his glass as if trying to make it ring. Ben doesn't expect him to. It had gone past that a long time ago.

★

They drive into wilder country, the land shouldering up into peaks. Cottonwood trees, and the dash of a river. Ben teaches Joshua to drive – how to start, how to keep going, how to stop. Not much need for anything else.

Still, he takes the wheel for the steep crooks of a pass. The view breaks open, and Joshua asks to stop.

Ben leans by the pick-up. It's a sight too vast to be understood, needs to be fragmented into line and ridge, weathering and rock-fall. There are small patches of snow that shine like honey glaze. The land at the valley floor is blue and indistinct.

A yell.

Joshua is shouting into the void, wordless, a vowel becoming another vowel, a howl. Exhilaration and rage at being alive, the sound skidding off angles of sheer rock. The mountain answering him, because no one else will.

Joshua's third shout dies in his throat. He points to the right – an armchair, salmon pink, perched at the end of a gravel track and facing the view. Though Ben calls to him, Joshua's off, dancing towards it in that kinetic, puckish way of his, shouting about just needing whiskey and a cigar.

As he reaches the chair, he places a hand on its back, and stops as if punched. Ben puts his chin to his chest, walks over. By the time he gets there, Joshua is sitting on the ground a few feet off, his temple resting on the heel of his hand, still too close for the impact of the smell.

What's left of the body is sodden and melting into the fabric of the chair. There's a glass tumbler slanted away from the hand, dark brown residue in the bottom topped with rainwater. Ben has seen it before – a couple on an arbour seat, at the end of their garden, looking onto wheat fields. One head still on the other's shoulder. Hard to know whether they'd chosen this way to go or not.

It's clearer this time.

*

That first day had been one of novelty, images from around the world in front of what looked like a fake background, meteorologists and scientists enthusing on bulletins. By the third

19

day, the crazies seemed to be on the money, and by then it was too late.

Things stayed on for a while, electricity worked, taps ran. News was presented by startled, unpractised faces. Some people had less severe symptoms, lasting longer. Suddenly unable to lift their limbs. Those red welts. A tiredness not just in the body but the heart, relinquishing life without question. In others, it showed up later – days, weeks, months. For a while, it was hard to tell who had it – the untouched walked around with a similar, calcified bewilderment.

First, they came to the cities. People wanting the shared experience of not having it, which turned out to be having it. There was talk of the air being cleaner out of the cities, so people drove there, while they still had the energy.

Bury your loved ones, had been the first message, on TV. *Bury who you can*, when it was just radio, then – spoken between those still standing – *bury what you can*.

★

They stop at a small town in long, flat scrubland ringed by mountains, violet rain blurring the undersides of clouds far off. There's a tunnel greenhouse on a homestead with old hay stacked in bricks and a rusty trailer. They feel for new growth underneath the rot, breathing through their mouths.

Maybe we can stay here, Joshua says.

Think it'll get pretty cold. Ben doesn't look up, or acknowledge the suggestion of something more permanent.

Eventually Joshua straightens. *This is stupid. There's nothing here.* He drifts outside.

Ben keeps searching. When he emerges with a handful of tiny zucchinis, he looks at the mountains. It's as humid outside as in the tunnel. The barn opposite is a couple of centuries old, its red paint peeling away. No birds.

Hello.

It's so long since he heard another voice that it takes him a moment. Then his head snaps round to the trailer, its door now open. A person in a matted dressing gown is there, short-haired, slight, leaning heavily on the frame. Ben's heart bolts into his throat.

Hello. The voice is very frail, dismal.

Joshua is standing on one leg on top of the wall

of haystacks by the road. *You look like you need a drink, friend,* he says, in a drawl, hopping down *Why don't we got to the saloon bar down the –*

Come on.

I don't care for your tone. He spits to the side. *I think you and me better have a meeting. With our pistols.*

We're going.

What? We only just got – he looks round, sees the person standing at the trailer door.

Ben is already taking his elbow, forcefully, and pushing him towards the pick-up.

★

They stumble around a mountain village resort in the dark until they find an empty cabin. It's cold and there's no fireplace. Joshua hasn't spoken much, drinking mini-bottles of rum outside.

He comes in, draining the dregs of one bottle and putting it on the table, his movements erratic. He unscrews the lid of another.

You should stop drinking, says Ben. *Or eat something.*

What are you, my dad? The words are shot out, dry and brittle. A flicker of regret on his face – they both know he isn't anywhere near old enough for that – is quickly flung aside.

Just trying to look out for you.

Joshua exhales a sour laugh and looks at the pine tree stencil on the wall. *It was one person and we left them.*

You don't get it.

Joshua marches over to him. *What the fuck do you know about it?* He leans over with an expression Ben hasn't seen before, lip curled, vindictive. *You don't know anything.*

Oh, yeah?

You don't know what – Joshua seems to get stuck on the word, almost stammer, and for a moment he looks like a child, – *what it was like. You just ran away. That's all you've been doing. See a flag, turn in the opposite direction.* He mimes, has become theatrical. *Pretend it never happened.* His voice drops, and the next words are delivered with relish. *You're a fucking coward.*

Ben tries to focus on his breathing. *Sit down.*

No.

Josh, will you sit down, for fuck's sake?

Something in his tone makes Joshua sink onto the couch, far apart from him.

Then he talks.

23

His first cluster had been on one floor of an apartment block by the hospital, once they knew it wasn't contagious. No one to blame except God, if you went in for that – or humans, if you really went in for God.

There'd been an odd beauty in how it happened. A gathering together. He and others helped people to the bathroom, sourced food and drink. It became two floors, and then he alone was trying to keep the whole block afloat, as the rest of the untouched alongside him began to grow listless, those bloodshot eyes, veins the same colour as that sky. They'd died, one by one, until he found himself on his own in that part of the city.

Those strange, gracious deaths. As if slipping into a warm river.

He'd driven out, past the lakes, not seeing a breathing soul for a while. One town had the striped flags that he'd seen in the city hanging from the windows – different colours sewn together or just overlaid, depending on what people could manage. The flags that meant *help us*. He'd joined them, and the scattered houses across the town had become a single street, compacting as people tried their best to care for each other. He moved the last survivors into one house, watched them go over a few days, the way they looked up at the sky with something like tenderness. Waiting.

Then I found a group in a real small town. No flags. But – you know.

Joshua barely moves his head, but he understands. A shred of hope in finding this band of people with urgency still in their bones, their eyes. But the tiredness, the welts, began to appear. They'd just been long-lasters. Everyone but him.

I started to just wish it would come. The looks that had been comradeship turned to resentment.

That your last one?

He shakes his head. He looks at his palms. *A kid wandered across the road in front of me. Up by the border. She wouldn't talk to me but I followed her.* His voice begins to edge away from him, as he pictures the schoolhouse by the Lutheran church, the flags half-fallen away. *Eight kids,* he says. The eldest had been twelve, trying to look after the others. She'd lasted longest, and he'd held her hand for hours after she'd gone. Her chipped, yellow-painted nails.

I'm not doing that any more. The words sail out on the old weariness he used to think must be the start. But it wasn't that blessing – it was the unfathomable weight of holding so many hands, seeing the red-veined eyes lose their shine. The monumental effort it took to know a new group of people, only for them to all die on him. *I can't.*

★

After that, Joshua doesn't demand anything.

He uses each town as a library, comes back with books tucked under his arm, along with supplies. Brings cartons of chocolate cereal, has stopped telling Ben to use a bowl. *You're disgusting. Aren't they stale now?* he says, as Ben sticks his hand in the box. *A little,* says Ben. *You're one to talk.* Nodding at the open jam jar, Joshua's fingers.

Two succulents still going strong are placed in the cup holders. Joshua samples colognes, smelling of apple or sandalwood. Starts wearing a thumb ring, tribal necklaces. Silver eyeliner. He finds a mandolin, and a travel chess set, on which he lets Ben teach him before hustling him in five minutes.

He's found several different recordings of the French piano piece, speaks of tone and interpretation as they listen, playing the air with his fingers.

★

I miss my brother, Joshua says.

He'd asked to see the sea. They'd both gone in, yelling with horror and delight at the cold. Now they've made a fire and sit opposite each other on driftwood, toasting crabs on sticks like s'mores.

He older or younger? Ben asks. Tries not to replay the memory of Joshua removing his T-shirt, of the beaded turquoise necklace against his clavicle.

Older. By seven minutes. He tosses the last crab shell aside, licks his thumb. *We were twins.*

The sudden mirage of not one but two of these young men in front of him. *Identical?* he asks.

In looks, yeah, but we both went out of our way to be different. He shaved his head, became a vegan, liked numbers. A small, self-conscious laugh, knowing it throws him into fresh relief. He puts his palms out to the fire.

The wind's picking up.

Do you have photos of them? Joshua says. *Your daughter and your wife?*

He shakes his head. *No.* He'd had hundreds, videos and audio messages too. *Daddy I love you more than the sun!*

A white pelican flies overhead, black-tipped wings and pale orange beak.

We were separated, he says.

They'd only been gone three weeks. His marriage had become bleak, untenable, reduced to a pattern of misunderstandings and arguments. But Hannah taking a job, and their daughter, so far away had never been part of the deal. Frankie had already got used to talking to him on screens every other day, only seeing his smiles – and not his fingers, jabbing into the underside of his thigh with the loss of her.

They hadn't bothered to get a landline. When he could get anything on his phone, he waited for the flood of messages – friends, family, anyone – that never arrived. After hitching across two states and breaking into their apartment, he found them, curled up together on the couch, only just blue. Sat there for a day, before wrapping them in a quilt. Returned to his city blind with grief.

Joshua leans back on his hands, looks up at the

half-moon. The firelight curves along his jawline. *I keep asking myself,* he says. *Why am I still here?*

Why are you?

No reason. Ben speaks kindly enough. *We're not special.*

Speak for yourself. Joshua remains deadpan for a moment, his eyes still on the sky. Then, the tiniest smile.

Ben laughs, the silent kind through his nose, but keeps looking over the fire at him anyway.

★

They head south. The coast is toothed into black basalt, the sea made into its most primal self, before mist comes in and smudges everything.

Joshua asks Ben for capital cities, state capitals, order of presidents, the world's tallest mountain, deepest ocean. Spends hours fiddling around with the mandolin. Plays metal songs, tunes he's picked up from the CDs, a Spanish lullaby his mom taught him. *Luna, lunita cascabelera.* Takes requests. He holds out the cereal box for Ben, and picks up sun cream for him.

You need to look after your freckles, he says.

Pumpkin fields. Evergreens. A handwritten sign for pick-your-own blueberries. They leave with purple-stained hands and mouths, a little hysterical. Dappled sun and redwoods. Mist again, and rain. A roadside stall with sodden cartons of homemade granola, next to a trailer with *STAY POSITIVE* written in yellow tape.

Joshua likes the sea, the open air. Ben says they can camp – it's warm enough – and goes to find supplies, leaving Joshua gathering driftwood.

When he returns, there's a motorbike at an angle by the edge of the car park. On the dunes, a man is talking to Joshua.

Joshua turns towards Ben as he approaches, his face animated. *This is Lewis.*

He's a lean, taut-faced white man in his fifties. Fit for his age. Wearing a thin brown leather jacket and fingerless motorbike gloves. He smiles, puts his hand out. *How's it going? Nice to see some walkers and talkers out on the road.* A Southern accent, musical.

Ben just nods.

Lewis lowers his hand. *I won't encroach on your time. I know how it is.*

It's fine, says Joshua. *Stay. We have bourbon.*

Well, if you're sure, says Lewis. He puts his hand

in the inside pocket of his jacket. *I can offer a peace token in the form of a peace toke. One thing for the dead – they certainly left a legacy of wonderful intoxicants to help us meditate on the future of humanity.*

They sit around the fire. Lewis is a man who likes the sound of his own voice. He talks about his travels to Cambodia and Laos, crossing some central Asian border with an old passport. Ben wonders how much he's making up.

He takes a couple of drags on the joint, though he's never been a fan. And someone should stay alert – Joshua is obviously an old hand. He seems lighter for a new presence, and Ben can't help resenting it. The balance has tilted.

Joshua asks a question, and at the same time claps a hand on his leg, lifts the ankle of his jeans up to scratch it. Lewis doesn't stop talking but Ben sees him register the glimpse of pale pink circle on Joshua's calf.

A little while later, Joshua stands, teeters slightly. *Gotta take a piss.* He grins. *That stuff is heavy.*

Lewis watches him go with a benevolent air.

Ben takes a long swig of the bourbon, only half-listening to him wind up his anecdote.

So, Lewis says. *When are you gonna do it?*

Excuse me?

The man reclines on one elbow, clasps his hands, his manner confiding. *I saw his leg. You and me both know there's only one way he's headed.* He looks gallingly genuine. *You're not going to make it easier for him?*

Ben stares at him. *What the fuck are you saying?*

Lewis scratches his nose, looks unperturbed. *How many have you watched die? He's slowing you down. Might as well save the resources for those that have a chance.*

Are you serious? The endless aisles of canned food, the silent houses.

He casts Ben a shrewd, near-amused gaze. *Haven't you seen the clusters? Still plenty of them hanging on.*

We haven't been looking for them. Ben lurches abruptly to his feet.

Lewis looks up at him. *If you need an instrument, say the word. Make it quick and easy for both of you.* His voice is gentle. *He wouldn't feel a thing.*

A scrap of sung melody. Joshua is coming

back over the dunes, arms out, fingers brushing the beachgrass.

Get the fuck out of here, Ben says.

Lewis is still for a moment, before unhurriedly getting up, wiping sand from his hands. *Alright, man. Just trying to help a brother out.*

Joshua has picked up on their tone, if not the words themselves. He looks between them, smile fading.

May wellness be within you, Lewis says to both of them, with dryness. He walks up towards his motorbike, rolling his shoulders back. Raises a hand without turning round as he disappears into the dark.

We could have had company, Joshua says, shovelling chips into his mouth.

They're driving south again, in the opposite direction to the motorbike. Ben's mind is still flared, violent, playing through the reactions he should've had, though he's never been that sort of person.

Trust me, you didn't want his.

The canyon road twists, darkness on either side. Rocks have fallen, and he swerves round them almost too late.

You guys get into an argument?
Yeah.
What about?

He focuses on the central markings on the road.

Joshua is still looking at him. *About me?*

He imagines what that man might have done to him. How.

Joshua lays a hand along his window ledge, taps languidly. Loosened by the weed. *Still hungry,* he says, and lets out an unselfconscious sigh. *You didn't have to worry,* he says. *I'm not going anywhere.*

There's a deep, plangent pain in Ben's gut. He stops in the middle of the road and yanks up the handbrake, gets out, over the barrier, into the scrub.

Ben. Joshua is calling. *What the fuck.*

He bends down, thinking he's going to throw up. Cool air on his neck. Joshua is singing one of the country songs they've listened to. He straightens again, tips his face up to the night sky. The moon is gauzy and low.

When he comes back a few minutes later, Joshua is standing in front of the soft orb of the headlights, making curved silhouettes with his arms onto the road. He lowers them as he sees Ben. Looks vulnerable, diaphanous, as if Ben could put his hands right through him. *Do you want me to go now?*

No, says Ben, the word long, shorn of all armour. He doesn't give himself time to hesitate. He steps right up to him, puts a hand on his waist, and kisses him. Just one kiss, before he lets go.

Joshua looks at him with a bemused expression. There's not a whisper of breath from either of them, and Ben feels a small, rising panic, wants to run.

Then Joshua smiles. It's sudden, distilled, makes the dreamlike road real once more, and the atoms of Ben's body settle in a new way. He kisses him again, and Joshua's mouth becomes jagged breaths, uncontrollable giggles. He slaps a hand to his forehead. *I'm so stoned.* He lowers his forehead on Ben's shoulder.

Yep, says Ben. *You are.*

Joshua holds onto him, shaking, helpless, and at some moment that Ben can't pinpoint, his laughter has muddied into heaving sobs, and Ben knows it's the relief of touching another human and being able to grieve.

He allows himself to do the same.

★

Joshua sleeps with his arms wrapped round himself, a frown line between his eyes. His breath short and concentrated.

They found a house up in the hills, the front door open. The bedroom smells of long-dead flowers and musty carpet, nothing more. A painting of a blue jay feather above their heads.

Ben watches the dreams rise in Joshua's face – a pulse in his temple, jaw tense, eyes darting behind his eyelids. His arm moves suddenly, as if swatting a fly, falls.

His eyes open. Cornflower-blue.

Hey.

He'd been unsure how far to take it, but Joshua hadn't seemed inexperienced. The two of them had shifted around and over each other in the folded dark, not fumbling as much as they might have.

Morning. Joshua's still caught in sleep, and it takes him a moment. Then he grins to himself, puts his palm over his own face, coy.

You OK?

Yeah. I just – he looks up at the static ceiling

fan. *I wasn't sure.*

Sorry.

Didn't want to fuck it up.

Have I fucked it up?

No. He sends a curious glance over. *It's just... with your wife and everything.*

Yeah.

Did she know?

Yeah. I like both.

Oh. He looks elegantly surprised, even pleased.

Somehow, he doesn't quite dare touch him this morning. *Listen*, he says. *You know I didn't take you with me just to –*

I know. Joshua reads him, easily. *Friends first.*

★

They get right down to the border, take an empty place on the beach. It's closer to other houses than any Ben has stayed in. One balcony looks onto the sea, the other onto salt marshes and sinuous water. Inside, there are white leather chairs that Joshua laughs at, and framed posters of palm trees. Joshua places the things he's accumulated on the road – instruments, nail polish, candles – along the

37

kitchen counter.

They enjoy each other. Joshua is frank, likes talking about what they've just done with that enjoyment of the recently sexual. Likes making Ben blush, which isn't all that hard. Ben finds himself laughing properly for the first time since everything. Joshua is surprisingly strong. *Piano arms,* he says, handing Ben back his jeans.

Joshua sits on the beach from where you can see the curve of the city further north, fiddling around with chords on the mandolin, says he'd planned to study ethnomusicology, travel to Borneo and study beduk drumming. He paints Ben's nails with the dark grey. They walk through the sage scrub in the shadow of the vast concrete wall. Ben talks about his daughter.

Joshua brings the edges of the city inside. Slowly, his findings appear on the windowsill – a Mexican hand-painted pottery owl, an abacus, a whole Japanese tea ceremony set. He puts a Keith Haring magnet on the fridge and waters the two succulents. They drink expensive rum and eat kale chips. Honey on stale crackers.

Ben prefers the mudflats, the tidal channels thinning and fattening each day. Waders dip their curved beaks into the brackish water and sparrows nest amongst the pickleweed. A subtle place, next to an unsubtle, pointless one.

★

One day, Joshua doesn't come back. Ben sits for a long time, watches the sun split itself onto the horizon. Thinks of Lewis, saying *some of us do things a little differently*.

He knows of two places with pianos, had helped Joshua move the bodies to another house far up the street. He's not in the first, a boulevard with a high school at the end. The second is up on the cliffs, scaffolded, the last light of dusk making the windows opaque. No sound from here, either. He hops over the low fence into the backyard.

Joshua's sitting in the near-dark, at the black grand piano.

Josh?

He hasn't put the lid up, as he usually does. Just looking at the keys.

Hey.

Joshua looks up at him, his shoulders low. *I'm too tired to play.*

Ben understands within a heartbeat what he

means. He kneels down. Joshua allows him to shine his torch at his eyes, pupils shrinking. The extra veins, that different shade of red. He feels a numbing shimmer over his skin.

I'm sorry, Joshua says, the words breaking open.

Ben draws him in, cradles the back of his head in his palm. *That's OK.*

★

They head east again. Joshua has asked to see the desert, the saguaros. He sits in the passenger seat, watching the land become dry, scorched. His body is silent – no percussive fingers, no under-the-breath singing. Most of the things he's collected have been left at the beach house, but he holds the Mexican clay owl in his hands. When Ben asks what albums he wants to play, he just shakes his head.

Soft light on the mountains. A state prison and a wind farm. A roadside banner saying *THERE IS EVIDENCE FOR GOD!* At the meeting of two deserts, Joshua says not to bother, to drive on. Ben listens for his own pulse, feels only empty space.

It's a new language of grit and dust, where every

plant bites and the air has no moisture. Joshua
wanders, lightly touching the powdery flowers
of brittlebush. Ben is sure it's shock, not just the
illness that's making him so tired. Digs his nails
into his palm.

They crest the mountain and into a valley that
for a moment seems so peopled it makes Ben's
chest bruise. The saguaros are countless, each
with an individual stance. Joshua stands next to
one, craning up to look at the central stem,
where a red-capped woodpecker peeks from a
perfect circle. The cactus, looking down at this
young man's slant, the gently craned back, hand
shielding his eyes.

    He might last, Ben tells himself. It's been
this long. It might be different.

    A whistle. Joshua is pointing down into the
valley. A large complex of houses, fenced, glints
with hundreds of lights.

The site is made up of adobe structures, coral
pink and peach, jade-green. A white pebble
path snakes around the perimeter and between
the buildings. There's a large desert garden,
strange sculptures covered with mosaic mirrors,
a pool. A low hum that is wind moving

through plastic tubes seemingly made for the purpose.

Ben said that perhaps the figures they could see were cacti, but Joshua was right – people are here. Not marooned inside, clinging to life with reluctance, but moving gently, watering beds, looking over as they arrive.

Hello there. A softly-spoken black woman in her fifties greets them. *Oh, you look well,* she says to Ben, with a strange, tranquil wonder. She has greying dreadlocks and linen dungarees.

He is well, says Joshua.

She gazes at Joshua for several moments, then steps up to him and places her hands on his cheeks. Ben has to look away, cannot bear this shared understanding.

You are so welcome here, she says to Joshua. Looks at Ben.

You all have it? he says.

She nods, simply. *We're all touched.*

Oh, my God, says Joshua, as they are shown into a large, mustard-walled room filled with paintings, ceramics. There's a grand piano, polished brown wood, the lid half-up.

Oh, you play, says the woman, whose name

is Camille.

Joshua remains standing, but lets his fingers fall onto the higher keys, plays a limpid phrase. He looks up at Ben with an astonishment that he doesn't understand.

We had a piano tuner living here, Camille says.

Joshua lets out a sated, exhausted sigh, both joy and regret.

Had, thinks Ben.

Ben sits out in the garden, surrounded by desert broom and juniper. Wood chimes gently interact nearby. Joshua wanted to lie down and he couldn't stay in there.

Camille brings him a mint tea in a handcrafted cup, sits next to him.

Do you need supplies? he says.

She smiles. *We have more than we need.*

You've done pretty well.

A serene hum. *Life is as long as it is.*

This a religious place?

Not in the way that you might be thinking. We know our journey is short, and so there is prayer of a kind in the way we live, wash, eat. These are the meaningful things.

But he knows, even if she doesn't, that this

calm-eyed, hopeful way of living will ebb from her. That one day she will be too tired to bring her spoon to her mouth, lift herself from the toilet or the floor, and there might not be anyone else to do it for her.

Perhaps these guys knew more than we ever did, she says, nodding at the saguaro nearest the fence, which gestures at the sky.

She sees it as supplicant, worshipful, he thinks. He sees it as fury.

★

In the morning, he finds Joshua in the piano room, playing fragments of the melodies Ben has come to know so well.

Ben sits down next to him on the long piano stool. *How're you doing?*

He'd slept curved around Joshua on the single bed, listening to him breathe for most of the night. When Joshua got up, there was a soft new circle on his shin. Larger than the others.

Joshua lays the flats of his palms soundlessly against the keys. *I wanna stay.*

Though Ben half-knew it was coming, he feels the reel of the room. *We can't.* The memories of his previous clusters collapsing into one.

I – I can't. I can't be the last one again, he means.

I know. But I want to.

Josh, you know what's going to happen here. I can look after you. His voice is in shreds.

No. You did enough. It feels good here.

And it didn't with me? He doesn't care how bitter he sounds.

It felt good with you. Always. But you don't owe me anything.

He feels the tears rise in him like bile, looks away.

Joshua leans against him, thigh to thigh, arm to arm. Rests his head on Ben's shoulder.

He stays another day, but it's too bone-rending. The unworldly ease with which everyone carries their tiredness. The way they all embrace Joshua, who's the youngest here. The way he lets them.

He leaves Joshua as he found him, sitting at a piano.

★

He drives.

He drives aimlessly, turning, turning again, getting lost, staring at the dead end of a desert

45

track as night falls. He hits the steering wheel, the window, himself. He cries. Sleeps. Finds his way back to the highway, to the coast. The waves are high and incensed.

He returns to the same house they'd stayed together, the flat, distant beach in front, salt marshes behind. Spends days inside, blinds down. All of Joshua's things around him.

There is a huge, whole, lavender moon.
    He stumbles out, over the dunes and along the estuary bed, to the river-mouth.

The moon is lower than seems possible, its belly resting on the horizon. Sending the waves towards him as he sits on the damp sand.
    Salt on his tongue. He hears the piece Joshua played so many times, its suspended tremors, ripples and aches, the air teasing apart into fine strands.
    The waves are pink, rose-gold, metallic.

He goes into the house, finds his keys.
    Drives towards the saguaros again, the moon at his back.

Flat 19

Jenn Ashworth

SOMEONE MADE A SPEECH about her unique vision and incomparable talent. They weren't going to name who they were describing until they called the winner up to the stage but Eve sat through it with her hands twisting in her lap and the dread closing over her head in dark waves. And yes, it was her — she'd won, and it was thousands of pounds.

She went up to the stage and her lips stuck to her teeth and her eyelids dragged on the suddenly sticky surface of her contact lenses. She should have been pleased and certainly tried her best to appear so. She smiled as people clinked their cutlery against their wine glasses. She'd made a proper effort, wearing a good dress and uncomfortable shoes. The little award and the big cheque were handed over and afterwards there was champagne, and she mingled among the white tablecloths, nodding and making sure her face was appropriately arranged for photographs that would, they assured her, appear in their trade journal the very next month.

★

When the issue arrived at the office Eve stared at her own face on its cover. Who was this person, who had worked tirelessly on a project, enhanced her company's reputation and won a significant and unexpected amount of money? Were those really her own eyes? How was it possible? What had possessed her? She rolled the magazine up and put it in the bottom drawer of her desk. Steven would want to frame it in the downstairs toilet. Guests would ask about it. She'd have to make a joke or enjoy being the subject of someone else's joke. She stared at the carpet underneath her desk. One of the senior partners had asked to meet with her that afternoon to have a conversation about what came next.

It had been the same with the bread-baking.

She'd tried it once, as a mindful activity that might relax her on the weekends, and something educational for the younger children to help out with. The weighing and measuring would be good for their maths. It would kill a rainy morning. The dough was sticky and grey in the first few attempts and refused to rise. She persevered. It was a good thing to do. Eventually she got the knack of mindful kneading and the little loaves swelled and browned in the oven. She became so competent a baker that a return to shop-bought bread had felt like a drop in standards and was experienced by her family as akin to an insult.

'What, no loaf?' Steven asked once. 'Have you fallen out with us?'

Now she rose at five to put the dough in the oven for forty minutes before everyone else rose at seven to eat it. She'd have to pull things like this – prizes and magazine covers – out of the bag all the time from now on.

Eve kicked off her shoes and crawled under the desk. She lay down, her cheek against the expensive, regularly cleaned wool loop pile. She'd chosen the carpet from a thick album of samples that she'd been presented with last year.

That had been work too. Creating the right impression. She turned onto her back and stared at the underside of her desk. Her email and instant message alerts and calendar reminders pinged first on her desktop computer, then a half second later on her mobile phone. She preferred not to answer these electronic demands for her attention. And as she lay motionless, she noticed that taped to the underside of her desk was a business card. She quickly peeled back the tape and retrieved the card, got up and sat in her office chair to inspect it.

It was a tasteful card made of creamy, thick paper with deckled edges. A navy blue 'W' in an understated font. Underneath, a phone number, and the phrase 'professional assistance'. Someone had spent time and effort on designing and producing this card. Someone – a whole team of someones, perhaps – had been keen to give the right impression. The impression she got was of a company that was expensive and had good reasons to be discreet. That name! She crawled out from under her desk and rang the number. It was as she'd hoped, only better.

★

When she got home that night, Steven was beating eggs while watching a video of a man in a chef's outfit talk him through the procedure on his tablet. Omelettes were his new obsession. An organic, protein-heavy diet was good for the health, he'd said. And though anyone could knock up an omelette it didn't cost anyone anything to learn how to do it properly. The French way. Sometimes, when he wasn't looking, she did it herself, using a folding plastic contraption that went in the microwave that she'd bought from a pound-shop and was not French at all.

'What will you do with the money?' he asked her. He really was only curious. He had plenty of his own, after all. The prize itself was enough for him: evidence, Eve thought meanly, that his careful nurturing of her potential through the years of their marriage had finally come to fruition.

'I haven't thought about it much,' she lied. He carried on beating. In about two minutes he was going to say, 'It's all in the wrist' and wink at her and she might scream or break a window. She might lie down under the kitchen table and pretend to be deaf. She might begin undressing and walk out onto the street without a stitch on and start singing the National Anthem on the village green. But all this would take effort, and the little lie didn't.

'I'd like to reinvest some of it. I have an idea for another project,' she said, and sketched out the idea – using lots of jargon so he'd be impressed and stop listening.

Steven left the eggs to settle and started grating cheese. There were two plates warming under the grill. Steven didn't like eating from cold plates, or from plates that were only hot because they'd just come out of the dishwasher.

'And I also thought I could set up some kind of fellowship. A paid internship. For people who want to get into the business but don't have any connections. From disadvantaged backgrounds.'

Steven smiled and poured the eggs into the hot pan.

'What a nice idea,' he said. He liked helping people from disadvantaged backgrounds become more like himself. Isn't that what he'd done to her? *For* her, she corrected herself. 'Here, eat up. You don't look well. Did you skip lunch?'

He pushed the plate over to her and she picked up her fork gratefully. It was a very good omelette. Later, she sat in her car and called W to set the whole thing up.

★

W messaged her the address of an out-of-town hotel. There she would meet with one of their agents and he would 'take her particulars'. A small conference room had been hired. She'd wondered, as she'd parked in the hotel car park, if this would feel like having an affair. To have your particulars taken sounded wonderfully mid-century and could be a euphemism for almost anything. She marvelled at the energy some people had for taking each other's particulars in the backs of cars and empty boardrooms and in hotels like this one, during the day. It was happening all over the place, according to Steven.

The hotel was cheap-looking and drab, and the lobby smelled like old frying pans. The conference room contained a vase of artificial flowers with dusty petals and bulbous orange plastic stamens that did not attempt to convince. A man stood by the window, waiting for her.

'Take a seat,' he said. She'd have to tell Steven she was sleeping with this man if he somehow discovered she'd been out of work that afternoon. He would be big about it – perhaps even indulgent. Wasn't being mature about things like this what people like them did? Eve saw immediately this man was not the type you'd start something clandestine with. He was mild, neat-haired and wore a suit that looked bespoke. He gestured towards a chair.

'It can feel awkward,' he said gently, 'to start. But I find this works better if I just,' he produced a tablet from a briefcase, 'work through the preliminary questions, and we can save some time at the end if you want to ask me anything. Water?'

There was a jug and glass. The water in the jug had dust swirling on its surface and Eve did not touch it. But she sat, and he used the tablet to record her answers to a dizzying variety of questions, from her waist measurement to her morning routine to the various tasks she performed for her children and husband each morning and evening.

'I'm not sure that you need to know…' Eve protested, as the questions progressed into the third hour and into the darker chambers of her marriage.

'Everything,' the man said with a reassuring smile. 'Even if you don't think it an important detail, you just don't know what would turn out to be important.'

It was as if he was a policeman and she a witness to a crime. The crime of her own life. Eve risked a smile. Now someone would surely see why she was so tired – why the whole business of her existence was so unbearably relentless she'd rather just be rid of it entirely for a while. Eventually, they got to the end of his list. He'd never introduced himself. She thought of him as 'W' – a name like a spy, or if he and his company were the same thing.

'I think that's all we need now.' He flipped the cover down over the tablet's screen and tucked it away. 'Now if you could just roll up your sleeve.'

'My sleeve?'

His hands were still in the briefcase, putting the tablet back, then he retrieved a pair of latex gloves, and a kit for taking blood.

'You're okay with needles, are you?'

She wanted to ask the man if he were a nurse, or in some other way qualified. Did you need special training to handle a syringe? Even hairdressers would give you Botox these days.

The man's fingernails were absolutely flawless and disappeared inside the latex gloves. She complied.

'Sharp scratch,' he said, and filled one vial after another. Her blood was dark, and she turned away as she heard it squirting into the bottles. She thought of Steven, pressing organic oranges through the juicer on Sunday mornings, listening to the radio and humming. Doll-like, she stared out of the window and blinked slowly, keeping her face free from any expression of pain or disgust.

★

That night she lay beside her husband in her long-sleeved nightdress even though it was a warm night, because she didn't want him to see the little round plaster on her inner elbow. He'd made some kind of almond and clementine cake from a recipe book, and they'd had it after dinner, and because he'd baked, Eve had felt obligated to make proper coffee in the pot with the matching cups, and now she was awake, ruminating. There'd been something not quite right about the man from W's bedside manner. She began to wonder – in a paranoid manner that seemed very reasonable (in fact, the worst of the paranoia was in not being able to entirely trust her own sense of disquiet) if this man was altogether there. If he was, well, *real*. She stared into the dark, listening to the tick of Steven's alarm clock. He hadn't dispensed any of the usual niceties. No congratulations on her being able to answer all the questions so fully, no response to her answers. It would have been nice, she thought, if he'd commented on how impossible and exhausting the maintenance of all her various lives had become – to tell her he quite understood her predicament. Once he'd taken her blood – such a lot of it – he'd plucked two strands of her hair from the nape of her neck and tucked them into a little plastic bag. Then he'd rubbed a cotton swab around the inside of her mouth, declining eye contact while he did so. Eventually, he'd turned his back to her while packing his things away. It was as if he was giving her privacy to recompose herself into a person after the detailed autopsy he'd just performed was complete.

'All done. We'll contact you. Couple of weeks.'

'I see.' She'd stood, reached for her handbag. Her feet were numb after so long sitting in the chair and hurt once she put her weight on them.

'And where will I go, while it all…happens?'

The man had smiled again. He seemed to have no other setting. She may as well tell him she was planning to use the time she was in the process of buying to perform an axe murder or a terrorist attack and all he'd do is dispense that tight, precise little smile of his.

'Well, that's up to you, Mrs. Smith. We'll give you a telephone so we can contact you privately in case there's some problem or emergency but,' (he must have caught her look of disappointment) 'we've been operating for nine years now and never had to disturb a client.'

'No, that's not what I mean. I know I need to stay out of the way. But where will I live?'

'We give you a flat. Nothing luxurious, I'm afraid, on your current scheme.' He glanced at his watch and handed her a brochure and she looked through pictures while he listed the options for upgrades and instalment plans, apologising for the flat's tiny size and dated furnishings, which he repeatedly referred to as 'simple' and 'uncluttered'.

'No, this one is perfect,' she'd said. And it was. She'd felt the way actresses in films always seem to feel when they fall in love. A recognition, a coming home. *So there you are,* she'd thought, gazing at the brochure.

And now, lying with Steven, she tried to think of it again – to enjoy the feelings of desire she had for it – her own flat for three whole months. But the man himself kept intruding into her fantasy. The not-quite-rightness of him.

Of course. He was one of those. The thought came to her suddenly, and once it arrived it felt like someone had thrown a rock in her face. He was one of those *things* the company made. It would make sense – they probably didn't get paid in the usual way, so it would be economical to have the assistants administering the scheme. And perhaps it would work as advertising too. Give the client a good old look at the product before asking for the first instalment. She shuddered and closed her eyes, making up her mind to dream of the flat and not of the man from W, if 'man' was the right word for what he was.

★

Two weeks later, she was summoned back to the hotel. She braced herself and managed not to scream or vomit at the sight of what waited for her. W had done an excellent job; exactly as promised. The agent – the same one as last time, or another one, waited discreetly while she inspected it.

'Will he be able to tell?' she asked eventually.

The woman – the thing – was standing quite still, staring unblinking into the middle distance. She breathed, and when Eve drew close and put a hand on her arm, her skin was warm. She had an urge – an almost unbearable one she would certainly have given in to if she had been alone with it – to slap it, to push it over, to pull its hair. But she contented herself with tugging its bottom lip down gently and inspecting a minute chip on the front bottom tooth, caused by her falling from her bike and hitting her face on the kerb when she was eleven years old. She touched her own tooth with her tongue, as if to reassure herself she was still there.

'Your husband?'

Eve nodded.

'Oh no, I shouldn't think so,' he said. 'It's never happened before. Not in…'

'Nine years,' Eve finished. This one had definitely been programmed with the sales patter.

'Yes,' he said. 'Isn't she beautiful? The lab were very pleased with how she turned out.' The man clasped his hands in front of him, like a well-trained butler. 'You must think of this period – this next three months – as a kind of alibi.'

'What a word.'

'Yes. A watertight alibi allowing you to be absent from your own life. You can do what you want with the time. One of our clients wrote a novel. Another went trekking in Nepal. It's a once in a lifetime opportunity for a once in a lifetime experience. The time doesn't count. You're still there, for all intents and purposes.'

That was sales talk if ever she heard it, and she'd already paid the first two instalments.

'And what happens afterwards? To the…' she gestured uncomfortably. Was it rude to talk about these things while their backs were turned? Before they were activated? Was it – *she* – on standby, or was she somehow aware, hearing but not responding, like a patient in a coma?

'Hello?' Eve whispered. The assistant did not respond. Its breathing continued, soft and even and regular. Eve was standing close enough to smell its hair, and it smelled of her own shampoo – which of course had been one of the questions.

'Once the commission ends the assistants remain the property of the agency, I'm afraid. Your image and your data belong to you, of course. But the component parts, the raw materials. We decommission them safely. There's a decreation process and a recycling programme.' He was being deliberately vague and smiled apologetically. 'It is humane, though not especially pretty. Your data is kept on our system for five years, in case you'd like to book again.'

Eve sat down heavily and he pressed a glass of water into her hand.

'Some people want a closer look. Would you like me to activate? I have the others in hotel rooms upstairs. I can ask them to come down?'

Eve shook her head quickly, her mind full of operating theatres and butchers' shops and the lairs of serial killers – imagining and trying not to imagine the decreation process. The recycling of parts. She supposed everyone was recycled, once you came down to it. She'd read that the water in her body was a thunderstorm last week and would be part of a fancy soufflé served in a Parisian café in a month's time. Her suitcase was at her feet. Seeing one of the things was enough – having the whole team in front of her would only be like naming the pigs that were destined to become bacon.

'No need,' she said, picked up the suitcase and asked the man at reception to call her a taxi to Flat 19.

*

The name of the flat was some kind of joke. It was three rooms above an empty workshop – the type that would have belonged to a mechanic or a joiner but was now blissfully empty – in a decrepit coastal town less than twenty miles from her home. There was no flat 18 or 20, and no flat number 1, either. She wondered what the postman thought, delivering letters, then supposed that if W regularly stashed its clients here, like cadavers in cold storage, there would never be any need for letters.

If she had wondered how it would be to have this time, unfettered and untethered, Eve would have supposed she'd have spent it eating chocolate in front of the telly, catching up on some box sets, reading trashy thrillers, ordering takeaway and sleeping. The team of deputy Eves, overseen by the man from W who assigned them their tasks, and he himself overseen by a team of shadowy others, all connected with some vital technology somewhere, would keep things ticking over. They were all at least as competent as she was, and more so. So there would be literally nothing for her to do. Eve might have imagined long baths in the afternoon, getting squiffy on fizzy wine before 6:00 p.m. and not bothering to wash her hair or shave her legs. But as she had not allowed herself to imagine what she might do with the time – she hadn't dared to – when it finally arrived, when she slipped through that marvellous crack in the wall and locked the door of the little sea-view flat behind her, she found herself unable to do anything except sink into the little armchair in front of the window and stare, unseeing, out at the water.

At the southern end of the little bay was a nuclear power station. She had no idea how they worked, and did not wonder, only regarded its blocky shape on the horizon, sometimes obscured by mist. Once every three days there would be a test alarm that echoed out from the station, over the wide bay and the cold flat water and into the flat. At first that was how she measured the time, emerging from her inner drifting only to note the siren, wailing out over the featureless bay, the sound bouncing around sea and rock and beach, and disturbing her only for a moment before she sank blissfully inwards again.

Of course, there were memories that drifted in and out like the clouds that drifted across the sky. Andrew would need new football boots, and there was a presentation to prepare for the Lessing account, and someone ought to come and look at the bifold doors in the kitchen, which leaked a little in rainy weather, and Jenny was going to need a dress for the end of term prom and someone needed to write a cheque for Esme's swimming lessons. There were Gantt charts to organise for the team, and a mole on Steven's back that needed looking at. She should visit her mother and get her to do something about the fence in her back garden, which was sagging.

Each of these thoughts she dispatched, as if they were misdirected letters, mentally redirecting them to the appropriate assistant. The man from W had explained the natural human flexibility to ricochet a self between a legion of roles and functions in life – the way we were never quite ourselves, but always somebody's wife, somebody's mother, someone else's friend or lover or daughter – was beyond the current capabilities of the company to replicate. They resolved this by creating a team of assistants, all different versions of Eve, and dispatched each to their individual work from a hotel, where they waited until they were required. The administration of the scheme sounded incredible, but W's man had shrugged off questions. 'We have our own team co-ordinating things,' he'd said.

Eve sometimes imagined the assistants

sitting, as she was, inert and staring unseeing into the dark of an unheated hotel room until they were requested. But eventually the inner roar of thought fell silent for longer and longer periods, and she sank into the blankness. She'd heard stories of Zen masters sitting in caves for years on end, staring at nothing while the snow fell around them and their feet rotted into gangrene. It was not waiting, what she was doing, because she was not expecting or anticipating anything. Apart from the siren coming and going every three days and reminding her to eat something, she let go of time entirely.

★

The agency had issued her with a phone for emergencies and promised to contact her on it to arrange her debriefing and return interview. She'd left it in a drawer in the kitchenette of Flat 19 and it had run out of charge. On one of the siren days, disturbed from her unselfed nothing by the gentle wailing, she retrieved this phone, plugged it into the wall and looked at the date and time on her screen. Four more days. That was all.

W had been sending her updates, little videos and pictures of the Eves about their business: dropping the kids at school, presenting to her colleagues, sitting on the train with a travel cup of coffee on the table in front of her. Eve swiped through the pictures hungrily and felt a great and powerful love for them, these little parts of herself, granted agency to do their work without her interference. How diligent and careful they were. How relentlessly efficient. These Eves, she realised, were precisely what Steven had in mind when he'd picked up the girl from the wrong side of the tracks at university and ended up marrying her while she was still grateful and pliable.

What would the agency do, she wondered, if she failed to turn up to her re-orientation appointment, where detailed reports, video montages and online records of her various selves would be shared to bring her up to speed and assist her in making a seamless, if reluctant, re-entry to her own life? Maybe she could message Steven and ask to meet him somewhere private. She'd take him out to the beach. Buy him a bag of chips which he'd sneer at, complaining about the cholesterol and the carbs. She'd explain the situation to him. Point out what a wonderful job her understudies were doing. Perhaps he'd prefer, she'd suggest, to keep things the way they were. Perhaps he'd like that better? Was there a way of suggesting it that would make him feel it was his idea in the first place? Would he agree to remortgage the house and pay W whatever they asked so she could come back to the flat? Or if not the flat – she looked around desperately at the drab little walls she'd barely noticed, the cloudy sand-scoured glass of the kitchen window, the grease spots on the tiles behind the cooker – then somewhere else. Nowhere else. She'd walk into the sea if she had to.

Eve clutched at the phone, swiping and scrolling. It was hopeless. Steven would never agree to it – her having her cake and eating it. Or having fewer cakes or eating none of them. Or hiring someone else to eat her share of the cake. He was always going on about *authentic* this and *artisanal* that. Spoke cuttingly about his sister, who sometimes brought counterfeit handbags home from trips abroad and bestowed them on her nieces. He'd never let the girls keep them. *People can tell,* he'd say. *People who matter can always tell.*

She knew without trying that not being able to tell would be so humiliating for him he'd simply refuse to believe it. The agency wouldn't back her up. Would vanish discreetly into the ether along with the assistants, leaving her trapped again in the competent prison of her life with a husband who'd commit her to a rehab or a rest home or a sanitorium somewhere. Wherever he put her away, it would be no Flat 19. There'd be wholesome group craft activities. Batik and macramé before lunch, brisk walks in the grounds among some council-planted daffodils, then a group encounter session for the inmates to talk about their mothers in the afternoon.

Eve used the phone to write a text message. She sent it to herself, to the mobile phone she'd handed over to W so they could clone it for the Eves to use while she was away. It was forbidden. There were many clauses in the contract on this matter. But they were her assistants, Eve reasoned. Who else was she supposed to call on? W would not help. Steven would not help. She'd ask the Eves.

★

The Eves came at the time and place she'd asked them to. This was a surprise: she imagined that they'd been assigned or programmed or instructed not to know of the existence of the original mother. But there they were: she saw them on the beach from a long way off. They were gathered, huddled, almost, as if sharing a secret or gossiping about an absent colleague. She wondered what they were speaking to each other about. Or if they even needed to speak at all. Perhaps they could communicate some other way, some signal or impression passed between their dark heads like messages carried in radio waves.

Shh, they were saying. *Look sharp, she's coming.*

A passer-by might have noted the general similarity between this group of women, but Eve was not striking in her looks and a group of averagely sized brown-haired white women on a beach in winter was hardly a remarkable sight apt to draw attention. The Eve that went to the office was wearing a good wool jacket and sensible leather shoes. The Eve that existed for the children seemed softer, somehow, in her jogging bottoms and with her shiny, scrubbed clean of make-up face. There was an Eve designed just for visits to her mother: not too successful, not too downtrodden, always wearing the god-awful purple cardigan her mother had presented to her the Christmas just gone and ready to smilingly absorb another instance of artless passive aggression. There were another couple of Eves she didn't recognise; one in impractical shoes, a too-tight silk blouse and a pencil skirt, the other one faded somehow, less defined than the others and seeming to exist only to display a long camel-coloured coat and some expensive looking choker sparkling around its neck. These two had been brought into being to answer some desire of Steven's the algorithm had detected, no doubt. Eve approached them all, walking carefully over the wet rocks and sand. She'd chosen the beach as a peaceful, private place, out in the open. But the waves crashed noisily and gulls screeched overhead, tossed around by the wind.

Eve had explained the decreation process to them in the message she sent. She'd done it brutally and cruelly, assuming that their end was forbidden knowledge they did not know. She'd told them about the deleting of data, the dismantling and recycling of parts. She'd made it sound worse than it probably was, but it had got them here, hadn't it? They'd gathered, and they waited. It was clearly the first time they'd met each other. Eve smiled to see her internal conflicts made flesh: Work Eve could not stand to be too near the Eve meant for the task of relating to her mother – they looked like two different women, thrust together by circumstance, and it was clear these two would never be friends. But seeing them like this felt the way it sometimes felt to see the children playing together nicely, unaware of her presence. Being able to witness their private conversation and rituals – how they were when mother was not in the room – invoked a rush of tenderness in her.

'Hello,' she called, still some way away now, but hurrying closer. The wind whipped away her voice and she slipped on a seaweed-covered rock, hurt her wrist breaking her own fall, then righted herself and carried on. 'Hello,' she said, 'hello, all you lot. It's me. I'm here.'

Would they all also feel the rush of love she was feeling now? That gratitude, and understanding of their sometimes difficult and unattractive ways? They all only wanted the best for her, after all – and deserved much better than they were destined for. She'd planned to try to explain the situation. To soften the gruesome brutality of her earlier messages. To help them understand what they were and where the responsibility for living and directing a shared life as complex as theirs most appropriately lay. Finally, she'd propose a compromise, and ask each of them to work together on hammering out the details of it. They would have to take some kind of vote.

Let's be democratic about this, she'd planned to say. *Let's put our heads together.*

There would be some solution. Some rota system. Perhaps she could go back to the agency and give them more money. Take out a loan. Get each of the Eves to take out their own loan. They'd need to be more: the multiplicity of her could expand infinitely, Eve thought, giddily – populate a city with deputies and create one dark nothing at its centre where Eve herself could wait. They could (this last thought came reluctantly, and even as it flickered through her mind, she knew she didn't mean it, would never do it, would never ever give it up) even share the flat and take turns with the drudgery that took place outside of it.

★

Eve remained curious about what was left of herself until the very end. Curious at her own surprise that these women who were the best, most efficient and well adapted parts of herself would be as reluctant to release their grip on her life as she was to take it up again. Curious at the relief and — yes — even gratitude she felt as she finally reached them and saw, as they turned one by one to face her, they were all quite prepared and organised, each of them holding a large and jagged rock from the shore's edge.

Of course. Of course! They're going to stone me, Eve thought joyfully, and laughed.

The first rock struck her — hard — on the side of the head. There was no pain, only the sudden heat of her own blood swiping down the side of her face and neck like the stroke of an unseen hand across her skin. A blessing, really. Eve turned to watch the grey rocking surface of the sea as the beach rose up to meet her and the women, who continued to hurl their rocks, screamed to each other like gulls.

Long Way to Come for a Sip of Water

Anna Bailey

HE HAS DREADED THIS. Dreaded who would call and who he would be obliged to speak to. But it's only Thomas' nurse whose voice bustles down the line, all the way from West Texas, giving Ready the impression of a large, matronly woman with little patience for the excuses of men. This turns out to be true, at least the latter part.

'Come or don't come,' she says. 'Everyone here says you won't, and your brother says that's the reason you will.'

Ready scoffs. He can hear the unmistakable drag of a cigarette in the background, and it makes him feel mildly revolted, looking at his own nicotine-stained fingers and imagining someone changing his underwear and sponging him down with yellow hands like that.

Well, that's what you get, he thinks, and he directs this privately at his brother. Thomas could have stayed in the hospital.

Ready had always expected to get the call after the fact. A last-minute invite to the funeral, perhaps, or someone diligently doing the rounds of Thomas' address book, letting people know he had passed, without realising that so much had gone between the brothers in the last few decades, the death of one would hardly seem like a milestone to the other. So he can't for the life of him figure out what Thomas is doing, getting in touch now, unless... unless he's prepared to hand it over, at last. Well, goddamn.

'He signed a DNR,' the nurse goes on, even though Ready had not asked. 'Do not resuscitate. You understand?'

'Uh huh.' He is slouched on the back porch, watching dusk fall over the pasture, the shadows of the horses grown long and distended, insects like pinches of dust in the blue bug zapper light.

'He reckoned you'd say that,' the nurse replies, and Ready hangs up on her. Doesn't care for the judgement. It was the same with his first wife, Helen. She thought that just because she'd married him, she'd married into the whole sorry business too and that earned her a stake in it. Well, it didn't. Nobody but him and Thomas get to scrap over that one. Whose business is it but his if he's about to come up trumps at last?

And yet his little brother had been right about one thing – best way to get Ready chomping at the bit for anything is to tell him he won't do it.

Like a badge of honour, Ready McGowen wears the same pair of steel-toed boots one of his mother's boyfriends used to kick the shit out of him when he was fourteen. He was long-limbed and ropey then, a collection of shaving cuts, torn denim and bloody teeth, and while he hides childish scars with thick stubble now, there is still something a little lanky about him, like he hasn't grown into himself yet, even at the age of forty-four.

These days he only scrubs up for funerals and weddings, two of which have been his own. Mothers of the brides have sighed and said he could have been James Dean in a past life, if the rebel without a cause had lived long enough to snort his weight in methadone and get his eyes blacked at every bar brawl between Texline and Amarillo, which is to say he is handsome, but the kind of good looks you run into the ground.

Hundreds of raw, red miles out there, and still he felt like the wrong shape for the place. Got out and headed east quick as if he had the Devil on his heels, and maybe by then he did. It was 1995 when things turned rotten, or so his brother said, but Ready still remembers the boyfriend with the boots and thinks that the problem with rot is that it always goes deeper than you realise, right down to the foundations.

'It's been a bad time,' Midge says. Midge from next door, Addie calls her, because Addie grew up in Dallas, where people have next-door and upstairs and downstairs neighbours, although Midge lives about a mile out from the McGowen property. It bothers Ready that his wife keeps saying this, like she has not adjusted to living out here, between the suburbs and the prairie. Like she does not especially intend to.

'It's been a bad time for a long time now,' Addie agrees, pouring three glasses of nameless red wine out of the box on the kitchen counter. She hands one off to Ready without looking at him on her way back to the couch. 'We got war and pestilence checked off, and famine is on its way, you bet, judging by the gas prices.' She jabs a finger at Midge with a kind of manic glee. 'And you know what comes next.'

Ready rolls his eyes. He finds this kind of talk exhausting – leave that to the preppers on Route 380, that's what he thinks, buying up their clean water filters and .44 calibres. 'What, if the end times come around, you gonna eat bullets?' he'd made the mistake of saying once and gotten a hole through his windshield for his troubles.

'Might be going away for a time,' he announces, and Addie looks up sharply. The sun is setting through the west window, collecting in the corners of photo frames and making her mousy hair look briefly burnished. The living room is all slices of orange light. The cross above the TV drips its shadow down the wall.

'First I'm hearing of it,' Addie says.

'Because it's the first I'm telling it.'

'Where you headed?' Midge asks, always eager to diffuse tension, to play Addie's gallant protector. Took one look at Ready the day they moved in and got a notion in her head that his wife needed protecting.

'Haring,' he says. 'Two or three days maybe, there and back.'

Addie raises her drawn-on eyebrows. 'Your brother's out that way. How long's it been since you last seen him?'

Later, Ready rolls over in bed and does not speak to her.

He sets out early, night still caught between the truckstops and the car dealerships like dregs in the bottom of a wine glass. Daylight is marked by how faint the neon grows as the interstate carries him further from the metroplex, goodbye to Braums and Dairy Queen. Past Decatur it's just miles and billboards. *DIRT 4 SALE. GOD LOVES YOU!!!! A HEART BEATS AT FOUR WEEKS*. And still, East Texas has always felt jammed up to him, even at this time of day when it's only Ready and the truckers on the road.

He grew up out west. Not Haring, but near

enough, close to the border with New Mexico. Prehistoric landscape, all arrowheads and hot wind. A man had space to breathe out there; you weren't just getting a lungful of some semi's exhaust fumes.

He swerves to overtake a church bus with Alaskan licence plates – you can get just about anything on these roads – and thinks of the old house. Built back in the days when men might have robbed stagecoaches in those parts, it was a great wooden pile, far enough from the highway that you didn't have to listen to the howl of traffic all the time. He and Thomas would go digging for fossils in the dried-up creek bed on the other side of the chain-link fence. He can still feel the pressure of that rust-coloured dirt compacted under his fingernails. Mama kept a jar of ammonites that Thomas added to loyally over the years, although when Ready brought her the skull of a bird of prey he'd found one afternoon in the scrubland, she smiled stiffly, and later he discovered it tossed away with the rest of the trash. It was like that. There was much between them, including all the space his father had left behind.

'You're the man of the house now,' she told

him, and she would send him to buy cigarettes from the gas station two miles down the road, even when he was too young to drive. Bright pink lipstick, that's what he remembers, and the acrid taste of hairspray gumming his tongue to the roof of his mouth, Mama humming Willie Nelson and glancing at Ready's reflection behind her in the bathroom mirror as she prepared to go out dancing. She looked like what she was: a woman coming up on middle age with too much dust in her eyes to see it.

'You want me to do your eyeshadow?' she laughed. She was always laughing at him, until things weren't so funny anymore.

He drives into a storm, rain like the report of assault rifles, the world beyond the windshield reduced to finger smudges. Traffic slows around Wichita Falls, the wind putting its muscle against the cars. The air coming through the vents smells waxy and cold, and the sky turns an unhealthy colour, just as Ready's phone lights up with a tornado warning for a neighbouring county. He barely glances at it. That's what you get, he thinks, close enough to Oklahoma that he could hit it with his spit if he rolled down the window, which he is not inclined to do.

'You really showed up to my deathbed looking like a drowned cat,' he can imagine Thomas saying, a smug smile breaking ground on his little rosebud mouth. How Mama used to fuss over that mouth – *cherubic*, she called it. Ready rolls his eyes.

A jeep looms large in his rear-view, coughing up black fumes, with mini Confederate flags on the roof snapping in the wind. People still feel a need to shout about that, huh, he thinks. Maybe it's easier for certain folks to stay mad about things from before, wearing a comfortable groove in old arguments, rather than face the state of the world now. More dying every month from some variant or another than were killed in the whole of 9/11. He can sense in his country a great sadness, the way grief comes on only after you've buried the body, although he is not sure what body it is they have buried. He can tell that he is part of a generation to which this world is no longer especially interested in catering – neither old enough to demand respect, nor young enough to preen over not getting any. Ready McGowen simply is, and even that feels like a stretch too, these days. Worn down to the quick of his soul.

When did the rope run out of give? Oh, he knows. When he and Thomas fell out. When Javier Des Santos stopped coming around, flashing his quick, dark eyes at them.

'You got blood on your hands ain't never gonna wash off!' Mama hurled at him that day, slamming the door.

Well, that's what you get.

The rain stops as quickly as it came on, steam rising from cars and blacktop alike as the heat boils the water back to heaven. He catches sight of the tornado on the far horizon, suspended like a woman's stocking from the clouds, and it lingers there in his wing mirror for an hour or so. Always been good at turning his back on things, that's what Mama would say.

He's hitting West Texas now, where the little towns are bone quiet, all the businesses boarded up or whited out, save for the gas stations and the funeral parlours. Around noon, he stops to gas up and grab a pack of cigarettes, while the strip lighting hums overhead and the cashier watches him listlessly, age and gender rendered obsolete by poverty and UV rays. His stomach groans for food, but he'd just as well eat one of the flattened armadillos baking on the edge of the highway than put a truckstop taquito into his body. Stopping was a bad idea. He can feel the exhaustion of an early start and too many hours behind the wheel catching up with him all at once, so he buys a Red Bull, even though the cashier warns that him the cooler packed in last week and they're still waiting on someone to get out and fix it.

'Whatever,' Ready says. He needs the caffeine. The cashier shrugs: it's a woman, he thinks, maybe, by the way her eyebrows are plucked to threads. When she wishes him a good day, he can see she is missing some of her teeth.

'You're too picky with women,' his first wife, Helen, used to say, although this was after the divorce had come through. She still liked to call sometimes, just to check that she was doing better than he was.

'Well, you're too picky with men,' was the best he could come up with in response, usually making good progress on a bottle of Jim Beam by that point in the evening.

'Ain't picky not to want a guy who only ever goes on about how hard he's had it. You wouldn't know a hard time if it flashed its tits at you. The veterans I work with at the shelter, some of them ain't even got arms and legs –'

Ready always hung up when she got around to talking about her work. Someone had to do it, he figured, and it was good that she did, but another sad sack getting dealt a shitty hand didn't make his set of cards any more fun to play with.

It's not like he has nothing to offer a woman, and indeed Addie had seen the value of a husband who knew how to cook and wash stains out and do any manner of repairs she needed. That was in fact how they'd met, him working with a plastering company at the time and being sent over to her apartment to fix a wall finished poorly by his predecessor.

'Your dad teach you how to do all this?' she'd asked once, when she was watching him from the bottom of a ladder, two glasses of sweet tea perspiring in her hands. When he shook his head, she said, 'Your mom then? Wow. I'd like to have met her.'

'No,' Ready replied, meaning that as an

answer to both statements. Everything he knew, he had taught himself, mostly by trial and error, and he had lost half his thumb trying to put in a new window at the old house one summer when the latest of Mama's boyfriends threw his shoe through the original one. Ready has bled and sweat over that house so much, there is enough of his DNA mixed up in the paint and the grouting that he considers the whole structure a blood relative.

That house belongs to him.

Doesn't matter what Mama wrote in her will, doesn't matter that it's Thomas' name on the deed. He is owed that house, and he'll get it even if... What's the saying? Even if he has to pry it out of his brother's dead hands.

He stands in the meagre shade of a gas pump and takes a few swigs of the Red Bull, before the sugary warmth of it makes him gag, and he tosses it away.

He blows a tyre somewhere before Childress, bald rubber spanking the tarmac and then flying clean off with a bang, throwing him into the hard shoulder. An eighteen-wheeler thunders past, blaring its horn and churning up red grit that sticks to Ready's face as he scrambles out of the truck to curse at the driver. The highway is otherwise empty, which would be a good thing if he were anywhere else in the world – less risk of being flattened, anyway – but out here the nothingness is uncanny. Dream-like, in its way. Just fields of pale stalks all the way to the horizon, still swaying from the passing hauler, the skitter of a tumbleweed making its way along the roadside in no particular hurry. It's like looking out at the ocean – he can see too far, and it makes him dizzy.

He calls AAA. When they ask for his location, he tries to bring a map up on his phone and the battery dies. He swears loud enough that a flock of dark birds takes off from the nearby field, and he remembers suddenly a time when he'd startled the crows in the back yard, and Mama had told him, 'That's the Devil taking flight. Even he don't want to stick around you too long.'

Ready twitches and rubs a hand over his face, pushing back sweat-slick hair. It's mid-afternoon and the sky is flinging out punishing heat. If he stays outside in this weather, he could get heatstroke, but if he just sits in his truck and waits to be rescued, he could end up being cooked alive. He scuffs his boots in the dirt and weighs up his options, while a vulture buzzard makes a wide arc overhead.

He could run the engine a little while, enough to charge up his phone and keep the AC going. He wouldn't need much battery to call AAA back, could always tell them he's somewhere outside of Childress and see if they can track him down that way. But like as not they won't, and then he'll have drained the truck's battery in the process, stranding him here until someone either charitable or wrong in the head offers to pick him up.

No, thank you. Spent too much time out west to trust anyone on these roads. He still has a half a tank of gas and three working tyres, enough to limp on to Childress by his reckoning.

It's slow going, like working a splinter out of a wound, but eventually he gets himself clear of those strange pale fields, covering flat, well-farmed countryside, until the town welcome sign comes into view. A Lone Star flag ripples on one side, while on the other, the speed limit has been graffitied over in red lettering.

UN-VAXXED! UN-POISONED! it reads, bold as brass, and who's going to scrub it off around here? Downtown's brick streets make the truck shudder. It gives Ready a headache.

This could all be some prank on Thomas' part, couldn't it? *I'm dying, come and see me.* What if he gets there and his brother jumps up from his sickbed and laughs in his face? What a good joke, making him drive all these lonesome miles out of his way, luring him in with the promise of the house that should be Ready's by right. But he's come this far.

He eats a drive-thru special that tastes vaguely yellow while he waits for the mechanics to fit him a new tyre, and he imagines fitting his hands around Thomas' throat.

Wouldn't be the first time.

When he reaches Amarillo, he can barely sit upright at the wheel. The city appears out of nowhere on the horizon, distant windows blazing with the sunset. What a place, like a child came up with it: sticking a giant cowboy statue here, an oversized fibreglass milkshake there. Balked by unfamiliar detours, he gets himself a motel room out of pure spite for the road, and collapses into bed without taking his boots off, feeling from head to toe like some long, withered root.

Better to sleep before this next leg of the journey anyhow. It's not only Thomas' company he's thinking of, but what will come before that – the highway slipping through ancient desert country, narrowing to just one lane either side at certain points, like it's trying to make itself small, trying to go unseen by the coyotes and the scorpions and all the things that know men and their engines do not belong out there. It would be a bad place to come off the road, with nothing and no one nearby for too many miles. Only a fool would drive it in the dark with sleep fraying him at the edges, and Ready, despite the testimony of two wives, does not consider himself a fool.

But what fool does? – his brother's voice this time. The sonofabitch always has to have the last word.

Ready dreams of split knuckles, of a throat yelled raw.

You can't smell anything in dreams – he doesn't remember where he heard that, although it sounds like something Addie would have said, back in their early days, lying in the hammock he'd put up for her in the pasture, while she read his palms for him. (He didn't buy into all that, but he liked having his hands touched with something other than violence.) You can't smell anything in dreams, and yet when he wakes in that cinderblock room, the vinyl drapes only half shutting out the sun that makes his eyes sting, he swears he still catches a trace of copper in the air.

He downs a packet of instant coffee mixed with greasy motel faucet water, and then he's off again, peeling out into a landscape that shrinks his car to the size of a flea. He has always liked that about this part of the country, how you can look in any direction you want without seeing a hint of mankind. Addie is the churchgoer, not him, but even so, he could believe that God lives out here, creeping over the earth, watching from between the mesas.

After an hour, he passes the burnt-out skeleton of a car a little ways off in the scrubland. Another hour after that, blood drying brown all over the blacktop. Maybe it's not God out here, he thinks, but something older, more feral, with a long memory and plenty of its own scores to settle.

Haring is about twenty miles north of where they grew up, him and Thomas. If pressed, he would say the town into which the old house was technically incorporated went by the name Ever Rest, although he and his brother never called it that. It was just The Town, because it was the only one. Same as the road was The Road and the house was The House, because they were young and dumb and their lives were so small they couldn't imagine being anywhere else.

It was the kind of place that made you think about the difference between living and surviving. Ready decided there was a difference, after he moved away from their mother.

But Thomas' apartment in Haring is not much better – a block of adobe lodged between a boarded-up building that may once have been a bank and a motel that looks like it hasn't been refurbished since the 1950s, despite the sign outside that promises: TV, WIFI, JESUS. Why Thomas picked such a dump to settle in when he's had the old house at his fingertips all this time, Ready will never understand. Except that perhaps his little brother, too, grew weary of mere survival.

The apartment is surprisingly cheery on the inside, however – walls painted cream to catch the best of the light, mason jars of dried flowers dotted here and there, a bowl of oranges on the coffee table that nearly takes Ready aback after his long, colourless drive.

'He said you'd come. We had a pool going; you cost me fifteen bucks.'

Ready had been expecting the matronly nurse, but instead he is shown indoors by a young man with a mouth like the curve of a peach and a mop of white-blond hair that reminds him uneasily of the field where he'd broken down the day before.

When he asks where the nurse is, the young man says, 'I'm looking after him now. You can call me Pearl.'

'Pearl? What sort of name is that for a guy?'

He looks like a doll. Like his whole face has been painted onto porcelain, and if you tapped him too hard, he might splinter into slender shards.

'What sort of a name is "Ready"?'

'I'm gonna use the bathroom,' he says, because he wants to be away from Pearl, with his weird name and his delicateness. To his horror, the bathroom door does not lock, and so he pisses with one sweaty fist closed tight around the handle. He has the awful sense that Pearl is watching him somehow. Boy would probably like that, wouldn't he? Trust Thomas to keep that kind of company.

When he emerges, however, Pearl is at the kitchen counter, busy trying to pry open a whole pineapple with his bare hands. 'I saw this video online,' he says. 'You're supposed to be able to get into it without using a knife.'

'Why would you want to do that?'

'For the fruit-on-fruit violence of it all, I guess.' He laughs to himself. Then, without looking up, he adds, 'You can go see him if you want. He's in his room.' As if Ready is just supposed to know where that is.

Thomas was often sick, growing up. He had a hole in his heart, which Ready pictured as a gaping flap into which he could poke his finger. It was usually his job to drive his brother over to the specialist in Amarillo, where the doctors were constantly re-estimating how many years the poor kid had left. One time Thomas collapsed from the heat, and they seemed almost pleased about that. Perhaps they'd had a pool going too.

He needed surgery that they couldn't afford. Thomas had been twelve and Ready sixteen, and on the weary drive home through the desert, he'd played Metallica as loud as he could on the fuzzy car stereo, and told Thomas to have a good long scream if he wanted. Thomas just asked him to turn the music down, in the same tone their mother would have used.

'You've gotten old,' his brother says, shuffling in his sickbed so that he's sitting upright, resting on a couple of sweat-stained pillows.

'You've gotten uglier,' Ready replies. He doesn't know where to put himself. Despite the buoyancy of a vase full of sunflowers on the desk, the room feels clammy and smells of blocked sinuses.

'I'm dying,' Thomas says. 'What's your excuse?'

The nurse had told Ready on the phone that while his brother had recovered from COVID, the virus had drastically exacerbated his cardiovascular issues. 'You understand what all those words mean?' she'd said, and Ready had told her to mind her own business. During the drive, he'd envisioned a bed surrounded by beeping machines that dragged Thomas' life out another day at a time, but the room is surprisingly empty, save for a fan shifting the stale air around and a pile of books on the nightstand.

'You read all those?' he asks.

'Not even started. Pearl keeps bringing them to me. Look at this.' He holds up a thick paperback with some French title. 'He says it's required queer reading.'

'Guess he would know.'

'Now, now. He's very good to me.'

'He looks about half your age.'

'How old is Addie, again?'

Ready flips him off, and Thomas says, 'Sit down. It's making me edgy, looking at you standing around.'

The only place he can see to sit is the bed, and he does not want to sit there. It feels like some ill piece of Thomas might get stuck to him, so he settles for a compromise, leaning against the wall. Thomas says, 'Well.'

'Well. You know why I'm here?'

His brother smiles sadly. 'I'd like to think it's

because you wanted to see me one last time, but sure. I know why you're here.'

'That house is mine.'

Thomas blinks at him like Ready hadn't said a word. 'I've kept it up, Mama's place – not as well as you used to, but it's in decent shape. I want you to do something for me first though.'

'I already drove 400 miles for you.'

'Don't kid yourself; that wasn't for me.' Thomas cocks his head. The hollows around his eyes are plum-coloured and tender-looking. 'I'll give you Mama's house if you tell me why you did it. Why did you beat me up that day?'

Ready huffs out a laugh. 'That's it? You know why. Mama loved on you too much. Someone had to toughen you up.'

'So it had nothing to do with me kissing Javier Des Santos.'

'Who?'

'That boy in your class. He used to prune our hackberry trees.'

When Ready doesn't reply, Thomas sighs. 'Go have some tea. Take a shower or something. You smell like roadkill.'

The water pressure is good, unlike the motel

where it felt as if someone was pissing on him gently. This is the scalding kind of spray that really hoses you down, although Ready is too distracted to enjoy it, pouring over whatever answer his brother had been seeking.

'I suppose you'll be wanting a towel too,' Pearl had said, standing in the doorway with his arms folded.

'No, I'm gonna shake myself out like a dog. Course I want a towel.'

'Don't clog up the drain with all that hair.'

Thankfully there is no sign of Pearl when he steps out of the shower. He feels a little less like spoiled meat, but he could do with something to eat. Dripping past his brother's room on the way to the kitchen, he hears the shush of quiet voices, and through the crack between the door and the frame he can see Pearl sitting beside Thomas on top of the covers, brushing his hair slowly. He has a faraway look in his eyes. Thomas is saying, 'He's never known how to ask for the things he wants, so he fixates on what he can't have. And he punishes everybody else.'

The journey has worn him out, and yet come

evening Ready still feels oddly keyed up. Alert from too much coffee, or from the subtle wariness that comes with staying in a stranger's house, knowing you do not belong there.

Thomas won't let him in again. He claims he is too tired and is going to sleep for a hundred years, and so, at a loss for what else to do, Ready heads across the street to the bar. A band is playing on a makeshift stage – some white trash bluegrass cover of a pop song he'd heard on the radio the other day, although what they lack in swagger, they make up for in banjo picking. He takes a seat at the bar with his back to them and orders a beer, and a voice to his left says, 'Oh, it's you.'

Pearl is sitting next to him, one bar stool between them, nursing a coke with more than a little Jack in it, judging by the smell.

'Who's watching my brother?'

'Himself,' Pearl says. 'He says he doesn't like me hovering over him all the time.'

'Can't say I blame him.'

'Does it ever get tiring, this whole mean-son-of-a-gun thing you work so hard on?'

'You sound like my ex-wife.' Ready takes a sip of his beer and wishes he hadn't said that.

The truth is he feels nervous about Pearl being here. The other patrons seem normal enough – a couple in leather jackets who are not bikers in the classic sense but probably enjoy you thinking otherwise; muscular middle-aged ranch wives with red hair right out of a bottle; men in wax jackets with their caps pulled low to cover balding heads, their faces moist and pink from too much summer – but their normalness is where the problem lies. Pearl, with his dainty doll features, is so clearly something else, and you can never tell who's going to decide to make that their problem.

The band finishes their song to a limp round of applause, followed by an interlude of tuning strings, the frontman clearing his throat and drawling out some joke that only gets a few laughs. There's nothing personal in people's lacklustre, Ready thinks. It's just been a long summer. A long decade, really, and they're only two years into it.

But when the first few chords tinkle out of the banjo, light as water, Pearl sits up straight, a grin splitting his ripe mouth, as he declares, 'This is my song!'

Ready cocks his ear and listens, abruptly jolted back to a muggy school gym where boys and girls kicked chalky balloons around the edges of the dancefloor instead of holding one another by the waist, although even in this there was a sense of togetherness. Ready had been sixteen or so, flask of bourbon stashed in his blazer pocket to pre-empt the hollow knowledge that no one would ask him to dance, at least not the person he'd wanted. This song had played on the speakers, he's almost certain. Something about a rose and a grey tower. The bluegrass boys are doing a decent cover, better than the last one anyway, and more upbeat than the original, even if it does sound a little crooked with a country twang. Ready wrinkles his nose all the same.

'What're you doing? Don't make a fool of yourself,' he says, as the chorus hits and Pearl tosses his head back to join in.

The bartender turns, some unreadable look startled out from under his heavy-lidded eyes. The others at the bar all stare in Pearl's direction, and Ready leans away, as if to say, *I'm not with him*. But then one of the ranch wives laughs — a deep belting laugh, like a man's — and joins in, and she catches Pearl's eye, and he points at her, beaming his way through the lyrics. As if they'd been waiting for permission, her friends join in now too, and not just the women, but their men as well, smacking each other on the arm, one of them cawing, 'Sharona, you couldn't hit that note if it was two feet in front of you!' The singer on the stage whips his hat off with renewed energy. Most of the bar chuckles through the verses – Pearl and one or two of the women are the only ones who seem to really know the words – but everyone raises their voices to the strains of the fiddle for the final chorus, and the banjo player must strum his fingers to ribbons finishing it off, the last few notes lost beneath a roar of laughter and applause.

Ready sits there feeling much as he had at junior prom all those years ago, which is to say, on the outside of things.

'That was a dumb thing to do,' he tells Pearl, as the kid knocks back a long swallow of Jack and coke, still buzzing like a plucked string. 'You shouldn't draw attention to yourself, not in this kind of place.'

'You're too negative about people.'

'I'm realistic. On a different night, any one of them might have knocked your teeth out.'

'Okay.' Pearl shrugs. 'But they didn't; they just wanted to sing.' The lights above the bar make his hair gleam gold, and Ready feels like a thief in noticing this. 'I think everyone's getting tired of being unhappy. Aren't you?'

Their mother's funeral was the last time Ready had seen his brother, before he drove all the way out to Haring. It was the weekend after Fourth of July, fourteen years ago, and Ever Rest's Main Street was strewn with tattered confetti crushed into the nooks and crannies of the sidewalk. In some parts of town, you could still smell the fireworks in the air. The heat was so bad all the flowers had wilted before the service was over, which seemed appropriate, considering how the day ended: Ready, marinated in whisky, driving his truck into the side of the little brick church.

'Mama would have been ashamed,' Thomas told him. Mama, who had drowned in the municipal pond – not an easy thing to do by any account, but, as she would have said herself, she'd never done anything because it was easy.

'Surprised they let someone like you step

foot in here,' Ready slurred back him. What he didn't say was that he had been ashamed of their mother too.

When they were still small, they used to listen to her getting into fights. She was a real one for bloodletting, used to beat her boyfriends as bad as they beat her sometimes. And it was during those fights that Ready would lead his brother up to the attic at the top of the old house, where he would tip over the hurricane lantern and cast a parade of shadow creatures on the blank wall with only his hands.

'You guess what this one is? Dog, yeah, that's right. Smart kid. What noise does a dog make? No, don't listen to them down there, you just tell me what noise a dog makes.'

In Thomas' apartment, he lies on the fold-out couch, night pressing at the windows, thick as molasses, and above the clunk of ice cubes calving in the freezer and the hum of the AC box jammed into the window, he hears his brother cry out. Pearl hurries from his own room and rattles the door handle a couple of times, his voice growing high-pitched and frantic, but Thomas does not get up to answer. Ready thinks about kicking the door in. He thinks about shaking Thomas, and then propping a lamp on its side to reawaken the old menagerie for him. But he doesn't, and come morning, as if to spite him, his brother is dead.

Pearl is sitting in a mustard velvet armchair in the corner of the living room, his legs drawn up, resting his chin on his knees.

Ready does not look him in the eye. 'Where is it?'

The boy only wipes his cheek with the heel of his hand and shakes his head.

'I said where is it, kid, I ain't hanging around. Where's the goddamn deed?'

'Is that all you care about?'

'Condolences and all, but it's a long drive and I got a wife to get back to.'

There's something slightly wild about the look Pearl fixes on him then. A kind of savage delight, and Ready should have seen this coming – the way you can see everything coming in the desert, the view going on forever – but it still feels like knuckles to the gut, Pearl saying, 'You know he already sold the house, right? Last year. He sold it to a charity in Potter County for queer youths.'

'You're lying,' Ready says, because he feels compelled to, like he read the lines off a script right in front of him. 'There's no charity for queers out here.'

'You've been gone a long time.'

'Not so long that folks changed their minds about that, I can tell you.'

Pearl pouts at him. 'Well, some people decided to do something about it, your brother being one of them. He sold the house. It was never gonna be yours.'

Ready feels like he's burning up under his clothes. Only two times he's ever felt like this before, the first being the day he beat his brother bloody, the second being when he drove his car into the church, and it seems like those are the only two paths he can see before him now. As if sensing this, Pearl goes very still, staring at him with big glassy eyes, and Ready's right hand twitches at his side with the memory of bone crunching. He can hear Pearl breathing fast. He clenches his fist until his nails dig into his palm, and then he pivots on his boot heel, storming out into the pummelling midday sun, crickets and katydids seething in the weeds as he slams the truck door.

He drives. The emptiness on the horizon feels like a wall he can drive right into, grit pinging off his hubcaps, the engine whining the way his brother had in the dead of night. Hefty columns of cloud tower over him, heralding storms that will probably blow themselves out long before they reach this county, but it makes him think of his teens, how he would race the rain up and down these kinds of roads with nothing better to do, hitting the gas pedal so hard he thought he could drive the car right into the earth.

He grips the steering wheel tight enough he can see his joints straining at the skin, and he doesn't think about it, the way he heads south, towards Ever Rest, towards the old house. He doesn't think about anything, except that maybe he still has a chance, if he can only get to the house, stake his claim, just like the old ranchers who built that place, displacing native peoples in a tide of blood. Hasn't it always been a matter of blood out here? He bled for that house, for his mother, who couldn't make up her mind what he was to her, and when he couldn't replace his father, she seemed to have no use for him at all.

He lets his anger run him through, too

focused on the electric feel of his own fury to notice the dead thing in the middle of the road. A deer, perhaps? At the last minute, as he swerves and the car flips over, he thinks he sees an antler sticking up out of the pulpy mess. But bent at that angle, it looks more like Thomas' arm had looked when Ready was finished with him, back in '95.

'How was that your song?' Last night, he'd leaned up outside the bar with a cigarette propped at the corner of his mouth, while Pearl finished the dregs of his Jack and coke. 'You can't have even been born when that came out.'

Pearl smiled. 'How young do you think I am?'

'Younger than loverboy up there,' Ready said and jerked his thumb towards the apartment block across the street. No lights were on in Thomas' place, and it made that side of the building look like a Halloween mask, blank space where the eyes should be.

'He's not my lover,' Pearl said. 'He's a friend. You know gay people can just know each other, right? Same as you're not hooking up with every woman you meet.'

'How'd you know?' Ready winked at him, and Pearl snorted.

'I'd like to think they had better taste than that.'

Ready was surprised at his own relief. He had not liked the thought of anyone touching his brother's body, worn ragged as it was, and this revelation made him feel more companionable. 'So what *are* you doing here then?'

'You weren't wrong before, I guess. This isn't the friendliest part of the world. You know how many fundraisers there are online for kids trying to get out of towns like this?' Pearl shook his head, and Ready thought he saw a heaviness overtake that doll face, something that made him sink deeper into his narrow shoulders. 'I guess what I'm saying is, Tom's been my friend, and I've been his. We look out for each other.'

Ready watched the boy raise the glass to his mouth. He had a thick blue vein on the back of his hand, and for a moment that he could not get a handle on, Ready pictured being a rattlesnake and biting down on it. 'I know what it's like,' he said, before he could stop himself. 'Wanting to get out of a place. Feeling like you've gotten too big for it. I know.'

'Oh yeah? Then how come you want your mom's house back so bad?'

'Because I made it what it was.'

'A big stack of splinters? I've seen it.'

This caught Ready off guard. He'd sort of imagined that Thomas kept his distance from the place, considering he wasn't living in it. It was odd to think of him still moving between those rooms, not quite a ghost yet, but getting close enough.

Maybe it was being startled like this that made him say, 'I could never get anything out of her. I couldn't scrape the love out of Mama if I tried. Least I can get is her house.'

Pearl looked at him then. Really seemed to look at him, as if previously he had only been glancing, the way one might glance at a cross at the side of the highway before driving swiftly on. 'You want some?' he said, offering the glass.

Ready wet his lips with his tongue. His mother's funeral was still on his mind. 'I think I'll get some water.'

'Long way to come for a sip of water.'

Pearl moved closer. His body was soft and soundless against the pebbledash wall, his mouth rosy and glinting from the liquor. When he was

113

only inches away, Ready didn't even think about it. He leaned in and kissed him. Pearl's lips were warm and tasted of whisky, and Ready thought he felt him breathe out shakily, like there was some relief in it.

'I ain't like this.' The words came out mechanically, as if Pearl's breath in his mouth was a coin slotted into him to make him go. But the next thing he knew, the boy was jerking away, his pretty face scrunched up.

'You're such a —'

'Don't,' Ready said, without knowing what the end of that sentence might be. His voice was hoarse as it had been when his mother saw what he'd done to Thomas, the way they'd screamed at each other like Ready was one of her boyfriends.

But Pearl only swallowed and turned and walked away towards the shadowy rooms where Ready's brother lay dying.

When he finally comes to, the sun has already set, leaving an orange stain along the seam of the world and a velvety indigo thickening the air. Ready's tongue tastes musty, probably from the airbag, which has left his face feeling tender as one giant bruise. He is numb everywhere else. He can see the broken glass in his hands, but it only bothers him in a faraway sense.

The truck is a wreck, crushed onto its side with all the windows smashed to pieces. He will have to climb out over the gear stick and the passenger seat, seeking places to put his hands without risking more glass in them, and then what? Not a single car has driven by in all the hours he's been lying here. With a shudder, he recalls the burnt-out vehicle he'd seen on the edge of Amarillo, and he thinks a whole convoy could have driven past and not looked twice. People aren't meant to live with this much distance between them.

It is cold in the wreckage. The wind that hurtles across the desert and plunges through the broken windows is no summer breeze, but the scouring kind that turns the earth on its axis. Ready shakes like a starving man. He never believed it, people saying your life passed before your eyes when death got its grip on you, but as the truck turned over, he had thought of certain things, there in the freefall. Not of his mother, or of Thomas, or even of the old house. But he had conjured the boy with the soft mouth and the

115

ways that seemed strange to Ready, perhaps because Pearl found no shame in them.

Above the sound of his chattering teeth, he can hear another noise now, and his ruined hands grapple blindly inside his jacket, feeling for his phone. Maybe it's Addie wondering when he'll be back, or Helen wanting to gloat – he doesn't dare hope it might be anyone else.

Splintered glass glints in the fading light as his fingers close around a familiar shape. He can't believe it survived the crash. He'd call it a miracle if he thought God held any sway out in the desert, but as it is, there are only the stars, spilled from one end of the sky to the other, and his phone ringing on and on. Clear as someone singing in the dark.

Green Afternoon

Vanessa Onwuemezi

A MOAN.

And I had to leave my chair, alone in the green   green afternoon.

The boy was bleeding from his side, eyes of gathering water   blind pools iridescent lungs a well draining out of life   a gurgle deep.

My hand on his stomach (exposed with shirt pulled upwards where he had dragged the body across the slabs) and felt warmth and trembling and wet, blood sweats the wound.

'Young man,' I said, 'my man.'

His eyelashes fluttered, a moth caught between my fingers   flash   the life's out.

I looked behind me. As if nothing had changed, the sky, green green and the grass blue as ever, empty but for the chair, a book and a chair.

I dreamed of blood from then on. Oceans of blood, rains of blood. It wasn't fearful dreaming but was painful and true, like the fact of death, living under the shadow of it, and now I had two shadows curled up on me like a shell hard and no give.

Around the lawn there was tape. My street haze of blue lights. I was taped around my middle, property of the investigation, indefinite. The blood remained, marked as it had pooled, the shape of an arm I could make out, a ribcage young and taut. The clean knife in a bush over there, was his.

Investigation heavy, investigation clueless. How was he here, in your place? How did he get into your property one afternoon when you were alone in the green? A communal garden, excuse us, understood, adjoined gardens private, still, you were the one to witness. How was he in? That's unknown, officer, the entry gate left unlocked most likely   must be a trail of blood from where he laid himself down. I hadn't deserved   the intrusion, officer, sitting with a book, and then the moan, yes the moan, and then he sank into the earth, leaving the pool of blood. My tongue is getting thick, woman, can this end? Might need me again she said, more questions. What's the matter with the answers you've got, I said, my nose isn't long, it's only wide.

I sought counsel: a number to call, 'phone consultation', appointment and   sit opposite him in a chair, half-smile (not too much smile) and nodding at my words and   to my annoyance   pencil grazing the paper while I spoke.

'Blood in my dreams,' I said to the man.

'Getting any exercise?' he said.

'I could outrun a water buffalo, a zebra,' I said, 'I have hooves man. What use is it though, to run about? With no direction to go.'

At which point he looked down at my shoes, housing what seemed to him obviously human toes. How stupid. My eyes rolled in, I could no longer see, ears shrunk closed. People blind and deaf to you will make you blind and deaf.

At home. The plane trees in the green were bent towards the site where   .

The police went quiet as cut grass in the weeks that followed. I called to see if I could wash away the blood stain. I was responded with a 'Who's this?' (Who the hell is this? they mouthed, but their mouths so loud I understood.) So I filled a bucket of water, Castile soap. The stain now condensed to black, with water and soap enlivened to red again and swallowed into the earth. The silence around the scene was unworldly, no fox squeal or chirp as is normal, heard my blood sing as it passed my ears.

'What for it?' a voice said to me. As tree and bush waved with the wind and branched   open arms. Some mercury in me expanded my veins and filled my mind, as if my own self was calibrated to that moment. 'What for it?' coaxing me again.

I'm going to find this killer and ask the right question then   and then have a why.

And from there (I'll say less by way of my deliberating, there was some) I took my hammer and nail to crack the shell, tapping for answers, beginning where the life had drained. My detective skills I took to be   as of yet undiscovered. If I were writing a note on this part of the story I'd call it:

¶ 1, death's power to invert all things

I photographed the site, on film, objects and edges blurry. But it wasn't precision I was after, not the faint details of the ground, but the mood.

How exactly had he entered? No matter, all I knew and needed to know was that he was here, the green space between the backs of houses.

I developed and pinned those images. One, the side-gate into the green. Two, my phone which I had used to call the officers, who did tape up and abandon me with the stain. Three, the site where   and the plane trees bent in mourning. Trees would recover, it was important to capture their bent backs as they were then, the beginning.

I looked in the local news, no ID of the boy too young. A picture of my street haze of blue lights. 'The victim had been…', 'The victim was found…', 'The victim was… liked,' from the middle pages. No capture, no one would grass-up, no one would give a lead and so the article ended with an appeal, and a full stop to say, 'We can all wash our hands clean.' But there was a quote from the mother, '- - - - - - - - -', as if she had risen from the pages and given me the first clue with her tongue, and what she clued was herself, and herself was to be found.

¶ 2, longest street marked by flowers

My street was the longest in the neighbourhood. Trees stand along it late spring to summer socialising, yapping their leaves.

I edged home one evening, all hat and suede and hands dry as chalk, grinding my teeth. Then noticed the flowers at the gate to the green. There were five bunches in all, of tulips, carnations and gladioli (or the sword lily, flowers in summer, unlike the tulip, but in many ways no more difficult to grow and should be planted before the last spring frost). I photographed each flower, and waited on my step for more mourners until just past sunset, none.

The next morning the flowers had increased by three, one pot of pinks in bud and bloom, peonies, white carnations. I looked closely at each flower in turn, there was a note, 'senseless' it said, but among it all no clue as to who the mother was.

I made a pot of coffee and with my book I

sat on my front steps to keep watch, made sure to wave a casual 'Hullo' to any passers-by without giving away that I was waiting for a flower bearer.

Night was quiet relief and in that deepest part, where time slackens, the darkness stirred. A hooded mourner made their way to the gate, sneaking soundless on white trainers, with lilies, a human shape but beyond that I couldn't make out, clothed in black and   oh   dark glasses, so as not to be blinded perhaps, by the loss.

I stood, and cleared my throat. They froze, and raised the glasses to look, slick of cheekbone and full lips, eyes hooded in shadow. I expected them to run, my hand gripped the step-rail like bird talons, but fattened and fleshy, heartbeat at a decent pace, each muscle in my back and legs and arms stiffened, tight from night-ushered cold.

Glad for me there wasn't a chase, nothing in me that was up to it. But I did walk down the steps cautiously, to avoid breaking the peace between   us quiet figures come down with the fever of spring.

'Could you tell me something?'

The flower bearer couldn't give the name of the mother, didn't know. But led me on a path through the night and   slick of cheekbone and full lips left me outside a pub on the edge of an estate, coffee pot between my two hands. Was she here in the drink hole? I suspected not. I was cautious of provoking a reaction to my snooping around. Hand pressed door and I was in, what was quiet from the outside erupted into my ears filled with the noise of people out late, so late.

There were those who slept on the benches edging the room, 'We're not sleeping, we're dancing,' they said. And those who filled the middle of the room in loud conversation and singing to music and etcetera. I hid my pot at the door. Tried to make my way towards the bar, blocked at every turn, so I aimed my order 'Brandy and coke!' towards the large ears of the ram serving.

My brother was a ram. His horns of bone-smoked porcelain curled to the sides of his head like the parted hair of Horace (the lesser known Horace, famed for his middle parting). My memory of Brother: fretting veins threading through his eyes, I imagine that his vision was clouded with red-tinted light, like the tint of every memory I have of him. These rams, the curled horns feed pride-blown mouths, the instrument of their volatile temperaments, self-importance, and   oh sometimes, bravery, wisdom and honour. Will this ram honour me with a drink?

It looked as though he would. A nod in my direction, and then to another bartender (son of a worm) tall and slinked his way along to the brandy, ice. Behind the bar there was a long tank full of golden-orange fish mouthing little Os in my direction. The ram and worm too mouthed Os of viscous smoke as joint passed back and forth. My drink was placed on the bar, and the ram transferred to me his brown (animal feeling), and I grew a chest width wider and found it in me to elbow my way through, sipped the drink, placed my money on the bar, beside the money I placed the photo of the site where   , and had my finger pointing his attention to the image.

He looked at it for a long while. I had finished the drink. He had toked the joint the way through and his eyes were red like my brother's, but he held a steady gaze.

When done, gazed at me and said, 'Who is it pictured here?'

'I thought you'd know, given the time you took –'

'You expect me to know the exact site where   , by looking at a picture?'

'No — I suppose it was the length of your looking that made me —'

'You're looking for the person dead?'

'His mother, it was a boy too young for an ID.

His mother gave a quote in the paper and said "– – – – – – – – – –".'

'Not much help. Could've been any mother.'

'I want to find who did it.'

'Who? Who?' Ram said, and laughed.

The tall worm chimed in, 'Who, who!'

My chest deflated, caved.

'Nobody will give you a who   man,' Ram said, 'you can roam around this estate all you like, ask your questions, make sure you're not known as police, is all we can say, and find the mother you're so keen to bother, you can't return her son.'

'But I was there when he   and can give her that.'

'Then go on. Come back when you know what we know.' Smoke thickened around his face and horns, crowd parted and my way through was given. As I left I grabbed my coffee pot, and felt I could go on.

'I can go on,' I said quiet to myself, 'now I can go on.'

¶ 3, Willow Walk

A side street called Willow Walk. I approached the estate it hummed the fluorescence of city asleep with one eye open. I'd forgotten what these places were like at night. No animal sounds here like at home (as is usual) not far away, but soon the concrete and brick took on the rough of bark, the bronze-green of moss combed by moonlight.

There was one light that flickered, I headed for that.

It was within a short underpass through one building, granting entry to a courtyard encircled by more, and more of them – buildings. As I passed beneath the flicker, the light went out. I was blinded, and the silence was blood again singing in my ears, heard someone exhale. Light on   flickering, at the end of the pass young man, two young women on a wall with heads bowed to talk.

I continued my step walked even. I tried too

much I know, and held my body too normal I know, for a someone walking around a dark brick-lain forest at night.

In low light   their faces glow and shadow of youth, turned to me as I approached. The first, her hair in braids and one or two slipped from her shoulder as her neck twisted, and hung there touching her hand, and the other, lighter-skinned and pinch-nosed, almond eyes and hair slick back and pressed flat a single curl to her cheek, and him, a cap and hood up, and tall and dressed in dark, and slim, and also looking at me.

Innocuous, 'Good night, isn't it?' I said, 'I don't live here I'm sure you might have guessed. I'm looking for a family member, a cousin, who's recently lost her son.'

They spoke in sentences broken between three mouths, like a ball being batted between them and kept from touching the ground. 'So, cousin, who you asking for exactly? What's the name of your cousin and her son?'

I hadn't anything to say then. So I stalled and said that I didn't quite understand and could they repeat and they did, in a configuration different to the first.

'Who you asking for cousin exactly? So her

son of your cousin? What's the name?'

I asked again, for the question to be repeated. And they repeated without aggravation, and so I asked, asked, asked the question circulated their lips for   enough time for the moon to change position. I don't know.

'For asking name your cousin, what's and so you exactly? The son of who her cousin?'

At this point, to my shame and a fact I am myself unable to forgive, I wanted to turn back. My feet had absorbed the cold and I was feeling as if   made of paper or straw, my stomach had filled with coffee and not much else since before sundown. To pack in the mission for benefit of hunger's edge? Yes I was considering it. Has worse been done on an empty stomach? Yes. Have some men and women been given the chop in a cruel rush of hunger? And things said that cannot be unsaid? And knives thrust that cannot be withdrawn? Yes. My error was just to think and to carry on the thought until I was leaving that place the way I came and back up my steps and into bed to erase the night so far.

At the heart of things, myself   alone, feeling unable to effect any good. Waning belief let my mind adrift on the winds of pale satisfactions, rumble in my stomach, my dining table, sitting, warm feet. The people in the pub didn't believe in the good. The death wasn't my fault, it wasn't. But the animal-headed people would have laughed if I'd stopped then, even if I never went back I would've heard them laughing on, and these three young ones went on and on. Until they arrived at a question I could answer.

'What's your cousin? The cousin name? Exactly who so asking you for her son?'

'My cousin is a man, son of the brother of my mother. The name, Bartold. The mother, in the newspaper, asked me for news of her son, who died at the site where   , and so died with me,' I said.

They responded, again between their three mouths, I caught the sentence I wanted to hear. It was Jahona I needed to find, Lucida Court, near the only tree in the estate.

Walking in the direction I guessed was right, water drop   onto my hand, dots onto dry skin and into the coffee pot, top up the dregs, light rain became heavy. I stopped in another underpass, my feet stiff with cold and ache, shoes becoming hard-soled and tight on the arches. I sat down, my back to the wall, and sipped at the coffee propped the pot by my side   listen   to the sour brown lapping at the glass pot with metal rim, keeping this rhythm that I call time.

Rain fell long, stretched threads of colour-white. The moon blindfolded in cloud. Found a mint in my pocket and ate. Through the patter I heard the regular brush brush of a tense broom, balcony on my left side and a woman brushing up and down the walkway. Up high. Crazy as. Like my ma, sometimes her arms are still up to it, sweeping the walkway on a balcony not dissimilar, where she keeps her flowers (and taught me the flowers), sweep of the broom regular with the sureness of night and day, sure as my brother coming home with a punch in the shoulder for me, wound up from a day doing whatever he did with his friends on the streets.

And likening this woman to Ma, how she sweeps, following some internal rhythm is how I got to this place? Brush brush, tiny papers fell from the walkway, then blown about and wetted, some bunched up in corners, and carried then further by quick swirls of wind. Those papers, I imagined one or two of them holding the names that I was missing, the boy, the killer, and with my mind nearly a blank sheet of white, my chin nodded to my chest, eyes closed.

¶ 4, just a head, light and cleared of thoughts

I felt the sound before I heard the sound. Rain had petered out, giving the air a crispness. And through the wall, and through my arse on the ground I felt a bass, deep, made by some other-world animal? A thought that was confirmed, a pair of eyes to my right, fixed on me with the clarity of the fresh-after-rain.

To my feet. Woman was sweeping still. Shook off the grog and paper that had gathered at my side, all blank, if they ever did have names. The eyes glowed red with a light that filled my own eyes, was all I could see cleared my thoughts, cleared my body away I felt my arms and legs disappearing. Enticing. Surpassed my urge to stay hidden. Without arms and legs, without a body I   just a head   moving forwards, no bodily fears, as all my fears were subsumed into the red, and no pains therefore. The bass was something akin to music, like none I've ever heard and closer I got to the source I saw objects emerge: red at first with faint lines, then darkening to firm silhouettes, boxes piled on the ground, door frame and open door, feet, arms, hands, necks, heads, noses put together into figures moving, slicking back and forth at work, at this hour?

Big men, shoulders enormous, forearms long and lined with ink, or scars, no heads hunched from heavy work and slow dragging bodies, but heads high, and mouths moving? Yes. One even blew a plume of smoke from his mouth while standing, back towards me, head turning left and right, a hand in his pocket he seemed relaxed as anything. Them shifting little bags of something up a stairwell was the reason for their walking back and forth with intention.

Closer I got, these big men getting smaller, and now I was closer than five metres and they were not men but boys, and some girls on the periphery, all shrunken in stature before me. Their skin in red light was so soft looking, and they became younger and younger, these babies' plump lips poked out, cheeks fattened, and a sweet smell wafted from them, like mashed, overripe apples.

The baby with head turning left and right caught sight of me, the lookout. I heard a howl, or cry, or moan, a call to assemble it must have been, because then they all did join the first, increasing in number, five, eight, thirteen, around a fire of red eye   car lights, steady on low, smoking engine, and heat exuding, deep bass a growl like I should call it mother. As I was surrounded, felt my body   suddenly too keenly, who was I kidding coming here all arms and legs? I shrank myself in as much as I could, they scratched at my chest, neck and face until I bled, and clumps of my hair I saw falling past my face as the plump-lipped babies drew and drew blood. I threw myself to the ground, whipping the contents of my pot into the air as I went, enough commotion for them to stop a moment and for me to say, 'I'm not police, none of my business what you're doing, looking for Jahona.' And it was tense quiet for a while.

I had courage enough to open an eye, sit up, and open the other. The pot had cracked like a scar across the face, but not broken and I hugged it in, and saw raised scratches across my hands throb and ooze.

'Jahona's at Lucida Court,' one said, finally. 'And you can't sneak up on mans at work and expect it to go well.'

'Fair,' I said, 'I'm her cousin.' But didn't mention the boy for fear of the reaction. 'Could you point me the way?'

'We're moving that way, so wait.'

I stayed sitting. They searched every part of my person until they were satisfied I was civilian, and returned to the work. There were others moving around them to buy some of the stuff, figures emerging from light and car exhaust and shrinking back into some groove of their own. They sold that   I guessed, I didn't say out loud even in my own mind. And one by one they sat and rested tired next to me, and perhaps because of my benign status, they talked.

Baby, sitting to my left, in green shirt, wore a studded chain with wings, proud to show himself pictured on his phone, a pose with jagged knives, hood up, showing it off for what? I asked.

They talked of the hunt, 'When we were young,' they said, and I, incredulous, knew that they couldn't have gotten any younger now and still be able to stand on stiff legs, any younger and they would have flopped over, rolling rubber-like on the ground, their talk turned to babble, any more again and they would have been returned to the fragile plane of the unborn, skin dissolved, each soul a tiny candle burning open to the air risk of being snuffed out by the sigh of a moth's wing, or an old man breathing through his whiskers.

'When we were young.' Opposite me, with cigar burnt down to a stub, continued. 'There was this boy, yeah.' And I said nothing, was this the boy I was here on behalf of ? 'Robbed one of our boys, coulda been worse, but he and his had to know we don't mess around.' He held me by the eyes as he spoke.

'He was your enemy? And his boys?' I said. Some laughter then.

'All a dem, except for the ones in here. And even then.'

We sat by car light with bass vibrating through our bones, holding us there to the floor. I began to understand some small bit.

'This place, you protect?'

'This rock, this mud, this earth,' they said. 'We keep order and fairness.'

'Revenge is the rules,' baby in green shirt said, 'one day, caught sight of the boy on road, luck, got us-selves together real quick, real gassed, real hyped, on bikes, and got around looking for him, found him hiding behind a wall.'

A burst of laughter from all of them, high and short. 'And then?' I said.

'He ran, of course.'

'You caught him?'

'Nah, the bus ran him down innit. He ran into the road and the bus ground him down flat.'

'You can't spend your time just doing that. Messing around with the order of things,' I said.

'And you're doing serious work around here? What are you doing round here?' The only girl to speak, pointed her finger at me.

They laughed. Howling laughter that was more and more a howl and more animal-like they seemed to me, in the red. Sharp noses attuned to sniff out each other, the mood of the street, or stale rhetoric and promises of regeneration generation over generation – it was a mournful howl.

Now was the moment. 'And, Jahona's son?' I said, and muscles tightened around the pot still in my arms. But they didn't hesitate to say:

'Our man, he was our boy, one of us.'

And I left a space without speaking, in the hopes of drawing more out of them.

'Don't know what he was doing in those ends, though they found him behind rich-people houses. But he had links all over innit. We'll know soon who did it, truth is round the corner, under every brick and stone. When we know who, we'll deal with them.'

He was their man, their boy. Boys are men, boys and men. These howling babies like a wolf pack, long-knived and short in the tooth, they did pack together and fit like pieces of a puzzle, like the network of roots that allows the tall tree to withstand the rush of a storm, the palest of winter droughts, the long dark nights of half-sleep without a coffee pot, indebted to the growling wolf mother, and each a father to each.

¶ 5, too late to see them

Me and my body, and the babies, began walking in the direction of Jahona. I was part of the pack for a short while, and felt the loose ends of invigoration, long forgotten, in the deep cavern of my belly, where somewhere a candle still burns a flush of youth and rage. I could see the tree on the approach, a birch so quiet, no yapping as is usual for a tree between blossom and leaf-bloom, no anticipation of what's to come, as if stuck between seasons' stillness without time.

A yellow flower at its foot, I grabbed it from the ground, dirt and roots in hand (Narcissus, to root us deeper into hope).

From a dark corner came someone, with hand out and searching for a fix that we   they could provide. And one of the pack went off into the dark to provide, before a shout clenched the air around my ears. I saw them, and more and more of them, there were police undercover and more police emptied from the hidden corners onto us.

This isn't how it's supposed to go, I'm told, don't make your sale right where you all stay, and while together. We felt too safe, and were sloppy. Undercover police. It was too late to see them, too late to dodge them. My presence I guilt over it.

One of the police came direct at me and politely requested my talking to him.

I began to sweat.

'A few questions, to follow up,' he said, as if we were acting a different scene from the rest. Over his shoulder I saw   babies dragged to the ground, one by one, and one tackled by two police, with elbow bent behind him then leaned into the ground by their knees, those blunt instruments, and barking from the shadows, teeth and glint of wet black eyes. They howled the last   nighttime gong. I dropped to my knees. Babies fled from this mud and earth they protect so much, or after faces pressed into it and munching enough grit, pushed into vans waiting, off to their cells. Two police stayed behind with me and I was ushered to a seat on some stairs. Coffee pot clutched and wouldn't let go now. Something divine about the vessel   wouldn't let go. And they asked, again no new questions but more of the same, never mind how I came to be in this place tonight, with babies. But questions for some self-satisfaction for them, that I could not grasp, answers I could not provide. And how was he in? What was he doing in the property   sir when you were alone in the green?

I was back again. In that afternoon, sky and grass   as ever. My sad book flat at page open facing up. And I sat in the chair, but could not embody the Me of that day, oblivious to everything that was to come next, and everything that was happening on my street, and streets away. But I've never been carefree exactly. There was always the tiny candle that could blow this way or that. I put a hand to my breast where I was keeping the knife that had dropped to the ground in the raging and chaos just before, to save the babies some bit of trouble. Beneath the handle a patch of sweat. I felt my fear more keenly, as prickles up my spine when the cool of the blade caressed my shirt, jagged edge scratch as the blade caught the fibres.

Hand on my shoulder. Hard stairs and smell of rain and rust. The police retreating. 'More questions   later.' Left alone I looked up, numbers, a list of names and buttons to call, Jahona, 65 A.

¶ 6, paper covered with the missing name

I pressed the button, buzz and click, firmly pulled the door open, up the stairs enclosed in glass held by a metal grid painted cobalt blue, reached the flat, knocked, door like weightless opened under my fist, a step in cautious, my scratches had dried but still throbbed.

Inside, a corridor, L-shaped. I followed it round to the left, dark, and light on in just one place, the kitchen. There she sat under single light hanging and curtains closed (remain closed night and day). It was her, Jahona, sat at kitchen table, hair tufting from beneath a scarf, dust bustling around hanging light like a cloud of restless insects.

'Thanks for coming,' she said.

'You don't know who –'

'People coming night and day, a blessing, sweet night and day.'

Her mouth curled, serene, and her eyes wrinkled with kindness, but was the kindness of yellow flower drooping, as her gaze never met mine, always looking just below   below my eyes.

Me, unworthy visitor, dragging my scratched body up there to give her nothing but news of nothing, and her boy's death, she already knew. And a vow to catch the killer – no effect on that so far.

She said she wanted to show me his room, back out into the corridor, her hand patting the wall for the light switch, on, and walls filled with pictures of the boy, as young and even younger than he was that day, in school uniform and smiling, year on year. The corridor had three more doors coming off it, all of them closed, and from the ceiling hung streamers, bunting, deflated balloons, like willow, vine and moss, in colours red, blue and green.

She opened the door ahead of us. In there, clothes folded on shelves, the best clothes hung on a rail ironed shirt and trousers, bed, pictures on the wall – places wanted to go, his friends – and behind, it all opened out to a field, hiss of the wind-grass bending to the east, and swaying trees in a line much further away as the field broke into a wood. A noise to break the silence of this place, and a clock on the boy's side table ticking a noise too.

'What is all this doing here?' I said to her, no answer, her back was turned and walking out. I followed, shut the door to his room, closed now to promise of the new.

'You have other children?' I asked.

'No,' she said. And edged the corridor, slowly, with one hand always touching the wall and the other pointing my eyes to the photographs and telling me his age in each, seven, four, thirteen, skin radiant of camera flash, of light, and a smile brilliant teeth. He was tall, I knew, popular with girls, and difficult to reason with, and messy with his room, she had tidied it most recently, and had been sleeping in there since he'd been gone. She didn't mention the field of grass, or trees.

I asked her if she had been exploring in there, she responded, 'Where's there to go? To explore, I can't, I can't expect anything new. Nothing of newness there for me to witness, can't see no green, only blackness made by this still time, can't leave these rooms and corridor, no forward or back, past and future was ripped away, and I'm bound to this silence. Maybe it won't be always, but it is now.'

Once close enough I cracked the door to his room, to double-check my faculties, which I had begun to doubt. The grass was there, enough to smell it, yes. I entered the room, taking her hand, past the bed and beneath my foot the crunch of grass but I felt her resist. She wouldn't go any further, her face, there was no curiosity in it, no recognition for solace, green and sounds offered by this secret field. Out of respect I didn't push, but crouched and took the flower from my pocket, shoved it into the ground. Its stem was blue, blue of the sky blue, in contrast to the green field. I shouted 'Goodbye!' and heard my voice disappear into buffer of open space, air, trees and breath of the wind, colours and sound as such, where I'd always known them to be.

The kitchen table. I told Jahona that I had a

hand on him at the end. And that his young soul was sunken somewhere into the earth of the green, behind the backs of houses. The trees were bent towards the site where he had died. Her eyes met mine for the first time, and were not smiling now but contained an ocean's depth, and water filled their edges. A bowl of oranges on the table, released sweet-acid smell of ferment. She had a paper clipping in front of her, I held out my hand, she gave. The local story, my street full of police, Jahona quoted, 'Identifying the body of my son, I looked into the face of silence,' and written across in pen repeated, his name.

She heaved in sobs and my insides sank like a stone into water.

'I'm sorry,' feeble, from me, 'I looked for answers and I've found none. But I will collect, if I may, what you have told me in tears.' I held the coffee pot out to catch her tears and it filled to the top.

¶ 7, whosoever makes the word, ends the game

My feet would hardly bend to carry me out of that place. Out of the flat, the estate. Was I tired or just weighed by unease, that heavied as

145

the night went on? Jahona didn't know who had killed her boy, not even a name or nod in the right direction – the police thought that she was holding back. 'I wouldn't hold back a thing,' she had said. She had nothing to lose now.

A pot of tears. Sat my arse on a wall on Willow Walk, hand in my jacket to find a tissue for my brow and grasped the knife a second. Electric feeling in my palm and fingers. The danger was over, but I sweated no less.

I went to the pub, hand pushed door and inside people much subdued, ceiling full of smoke and low talking in a stupor. The ram was seated at a table to my right, and caught me in his eye just after I'd caught him in mine, and, 'Ahh he's back,' from him, and others then turned in my direction, tugged at my sleeves to guide me to a seat. Ram's arm around my shoulders, heavy, my back hunched under it.

'So tell us what you found out,' he said.

'Well, I found his mother and told her that her boy wasn't alone when he went, and named the location where the trees lean over the grass and –'

'Some cold comfort for a mother then.'

'Yes.'

'And the killer, you caught him or her and strung them up?'

'Nothing on that, nothing.'

'It's not so easy is it, detective?'

'You said I'd find it out, what you already know.'

'First, you can join our game.' Grunts of enjoyment from the worm, and other men and women, passing around a joint oozing smoke. I wanted to drag myself out of there. Not play. The pot I'd left tucked at the door was a pinch on my mind.

'Can you turn my smile into tears?' he said.

Again like my old body on the stairs earlier that night, I stiffened in my mind and nothing came. How to make a ram cry? I recounted how I'd found the boy, details, how he'd moaned and tried to say a name or something while holding my gaze through water in the eyes. I said to them all   how warm the blood. How it had pooled   so much of it, it might have formed a tide, and then it had darkened to black, and since then I am submerged in this black and quiet night.

But he stayed smiling. I beat my fists on the table and hung my head, looked up and locked eyes with a fish in the tank, felt its gaze on me and mouth an O pulsating, round eyes and narrow face watching, while people around me puffed out smoke in similar motion.

I had it. I went to the door and picked up the pot, put it in the centre of the table so everyone could see.

'Your tears,' I said, and stood back.

'Your pot is cracked,' he said, and gestured to my clothes and to the table where the pot, half full, was leaking onto it, and had emptied onto me. I must have smelled quite strong of body by now, sweating still and desperate for an answer, to leave soon. The electric feeling spread from my hand, across my torso, into my neck and eyes, and agitating.

'That's right, laughing is all you can do, a tear has never left that face!' My dejection only invited more laughter, punishing eyes of fish.

'Whosoever makes the word, ends the game,' he said, 'I start with a smile and end in tears.'

I was ready to throw myself at him, but I noticed, just next to where he was sitting, paper pieces, each with one letter of the alphabet, A, B, C, O, X and so on. Amongst them the word 'smile' was spelled out. I hovered over the papers and then changing one letter at a time moved towards the wanted word. And talked out loud to help me through it:

'I start with a "smile", along the footpath I move and climb over a "stile", no animal, no ram or worm can follow me, on the other side I step on a pile of "stale" manure and over the hedge, a ram locks me in a "stare" with no sympathy for my bad luck, in his eyes he possesses the "stars" and I, drawn by animal feeling, enter his eye screaming, I'm thrown towards the sun which "sears" my skin, my eyes burning full of "tears".'

A rush of relief, opened something in me, short-lived.

They all got to their feet. I grabbed the pot, holding in whatever could be kept in with my hand. Felt the leak of tears over fingers.

'You had a fun night roaming around with the boys, I'm sure. Tell us what we already know,' Ram said.

At last I said, 'If I want a pot to be cracked, I throw it to the ground.'

They clapped furiously, breathed out thick smoke. I coughed, and as I coughed out of my mouth flowed yet more heavy smoke, stung my eyes, full of water and itching stinging, spilled whatever was left in the pot onto myself.

Back again. In the green back again. He was standing beneath the plane trees that weren't bent but tall   again, stretching to the sky dark and pinked with clouds, I could see well. My clothes and body damp with sweat, tears, and in my agitation (electric feeling) lurched for the boy and took the knife from my breast and shoved. Drove it in. Pulled it out and   jagged edge ripped out sinew after sinew like feathers from fowl.

He fell. A moan. This rock, this mud, this earth and run.

I ran through the back door of my house and out of the front, down my steps and street haze of blue lights and tape. And myself stunned. I ran with eyes wide, street studded with mourners and grievers and mothers and police, their round eyes looking back at me, mouths open glistening red, and faces contorted with surprise, mouthing the little Os.

Blue 4eva

Saba Sams

STELLA'S LYING ON A sun lounger, and then her book is wet. She watches the dots darken the paper as they sink in. On the surface of the pool, tiny blue waves ricochet out, the sun skittering off them. Underneath is the dark silhouette of a girl. She swims the whole length without coming up for air. When she breaks the surface, she puts her arms on the tiled edge and rests her chin in the crook of her wrists. Stella looks back at her book.

'Hey, you. I see you.'

The girl is Blue, a friend of Jasmine's from school. Her eyes are narrowed to the sun. Under her armpit, Stella notices a tangle of dark hair, slicked down like a clump pulled from the plughole.

'You the baby, then?'

'Guess so.'

Blue pushes off into the water again, floating on her back with her head lifted. Stella can't think of anything good to say, and eventually Blue lets her ears slip under. The cicadas sing in the background like a phone vibrating.

Stella's mother married Jasmine's father in February. Stella was twelve, Jasmine was eighteen. For their honeymoon, Claire and Frank went to Costa Rica. Stella and Jasmine weren't invited. When they returned home, Frank announced that he'd booked three weeks in a villa on the smallest island in the Balearics, to make up for it. Jasmine was over from her mother's. Claire had baked a lemon drizzle.

'Cake's for children,' said Jasmine. 'And I'm not coming.'

They've been on holiday for five days. No one asked what it was that made Jasmine change her mind and join them. Stella suspects she's only here to ensure that everyone has as difficult a time as possible. Jasmine knocks hard on the bathroom door whenever Stella's in the shower. She steals Stella's sun lounger the moment she gets in the pool.

'This is my spot,' Jasmine says, waving to the strip of shade where the other lounger waits.

There are other things too, little things that Stella can't prove. She woke up one morning itchy with bites, and discovered a tiny hole in her mosquito net that she was sure hadn't been there when she'd fallen asleep. Another time, someone moved her book into the sun and left it for hours, so the glue in the spine melted and the pages started falling out.

Back in England, Stella's bedroom used to be Jasmine's. Everything in it is either white or beige. There's a low bed, a rug made of woven straw, and a pale, angular desk beneath a desktop computer, the monitor the size of a plasma television. Stella had never had her own computer, before this.

'I don't know if that's a good idea,' Claire said, when she saw.

Frank only winked at Stella. She's at secondary now. She might need it for homework.

It was the day they'd moved in. Frank had already ordered pizzas for dinner, and opened up the shed in the garden to reveal an expensive-looking bike, bright green with yellow lightning bolts across the handlebars. If this was what having a dad was, Stella could get used to it.

In fact, Stella's school made a point not to set homework on the computer. When Stella found out about the holiday, it was the first time she used the desktop for anything other than video games. She looked up the island and sat for hours, hovering her mouse over the images. She didn't go downstairs again all evening, and Jasmine left without saying goodbye. The water looked so clear Stella could see the shadows of the boats on the sand at the bottom of the sea. She thought that when she swam in it, she'd be able to watch the fish drifting beneath her, an aquarium without the glass.

Out here, Stella spends most of her time with Frank and Claire, while Jasmine stays alone in the villa. In the mornings, they set up on the beach and eat peaches in the shade of a parasol. Stella climbs onto Frank's shoulders and dives off them into the sea. In the afternoons, they wander the dusty towns, stopping in cafes and stone churches to drink coffee or light candles,

Frank's camera swinging around his neck. Frank buys Stella little gifts wherever they go: a keyring with a lizard on it, a pair of canvas espadrilles. Sometimes, he puts his hand on Claire's waist while they're walking, and pulls her into him. Claire looks at Stella sideways, a little embarrassed.

In the evenings, back at the villa, the three of them sit on the veranda. Frank cuts slivers of manchego with a satisfying contraption while Claire mixes sangria in a big glass jug. Last night, for the first time, Jasmine came outside and poured herself a glass.

'OK, kids,' she said. 'Fun's over. You can all stop pretending to be functional now.'

Frank cut a slice of manchego and lay it down in front of her. Jasmine didn't touch her cheese. After some minutes, she announced that she'd invited Blue out to join them.

Frank threaded his fingers together on the table. 'The point of this trip,' he said, 'was to spend time together as a four.'

'Right. And how is that working out for you?'

Frank went quiet after that, and Blue wasn't mentioned again all evening. By morning, Stella had forgotten all about her. By afternoon, here she was.

Blue lifts herself out of the pool and sits on the edge, leaning back on her long arms to feel the sun on her chest. She spreads her legs like a man, not seeming to worry that the flesh of her thighs looks bigger pressed against the tiles. 'Fuck me, it's hot.'

Stella loves it when people swear in front of her. 'Tell me about it,' she says.

A sound comes from behind the dry stone wall that separates the villa from the farmland around it. The sound is like a tiny sneeze, or the extending of a plastic straw. Stella's used to these sounds by now, but Blue whips her head over her shoulder to look.

'No. Sorry, no. As you were.'

Blue turns her head back to its previous position. Frank appears from behind the wall. 'Damn,' he says. 'Lost it.'

Blue laughs. 'Am I going to feature in an upcoming exhibition, Franklin Royce?'

Franklin Royce is Frank's public name. Stella's never heard anyone call him that in real life before.

Frank comes over to Blue and kisses her on both cheeks. 'Only if you're very lucky, and if you keep still when I ask you to.'

'You'll be the lucky one. I'm far too hyperactive to model.'

'I've no interest in models,' he says. He nods towards Stella. 'Have you met my latest muse?'

'I thought she was your stepdaughter.'

'She is. But she also happens to be a dream in front of the camera. Unfussy, almost child-like.'

'That's because she is a child,' says Blue. She turns to Stella. 'How do you feel about all this?'

It isn't a question Stella's been asked before. Frank's interest in taking photographs of her only developed this holiday. 'I don't mind,' she says. 'It's fun.'

'There you go then. Your girl loves the limelight.'

In school, Stella's not one of the pretty girls. Her face is round and freckled, with a low, square forehead. She isn't particularly tall or thin. The limelight is a place in which she'd never imagined finding herself. Claire, on the other hand, modelled when she was younger.

Stella's seen some of the editorials hung up in her grandparents' bathroom.

A few months ago, Stella attended one of Frank's shows. It was full of blurred, bare-skinned women against a blue sky, and those translucent, dusty-looking bubbles that sunlight sometimes creates in a lens. His photographs were printed large enough to take up an entire wall on their own, and people seemed to be able to stand in front of them for hours, just staring. Stella knows her grandparents don't have that much space in their house, or that much patience.

Frank lifts his camera and snaps it a few times at Stella. She isn't sure if he's seriously taking photographs, or if he's performing for Blue.

Jasmine's voice carries over from the veranda. Stella hadn't realised she was there. 'Will you two stop treating this whole place as your fucking studio?'

'It was me who paid for this villa,' says Frank, 'and I'll treat it how I like.'

'Whatever. We're heading into town, right Blue?'

Blue pulls her legs out of the pool and stands

up. Stella thinks that if she had a camera, she'd take a photograph of Blue right there, on the edge of the pool like that.

'You wanna come?'

'Hell no,' calls Jasmine.

'It's OK. I'm fine here.'

Blue's hair is made up of tight curls that skim the waistline of her bikini bottoms. When she turns to leave, beads of water spray out from the ends and catch the sun.

Neither Blue nor Jasmine have a license to drive the car that Frank's rented, so they take the old mopeds that belong to the house. Stella hears the exhausts flare and then fizzle as they drive away. She swims for a while. Claire and Frank set up on the veranda and start eating tuna niçoise.

'Come try this,' calls Claire. 'Have you been drinking enough water?'

The salad has green beans in it, and the water next to Stella's plate has been poured into a pint glass. She takes a sip.

'Drink it all,' says Claire. 'Show me you can.'

'I'm not eight.'

'No,' says Frank. 'You're eighteen. Now

down that pint. Down it.'

Stella drinks the entire glass of water in one. She splutters as she finishes, trying not to laugh. By the time she gets around to her salad, Claire and Frank are done eating. Frank gets his camera out and holds it to his eye, twisting the lens very slowly so that it ticks like a clock.

Frank's camera is newly fitted with something called a Dream Lens, a rare piece of kit that he bought specifically for the intense sunshine of the holiday. A month before, he'd sent the lens to Japan, along with his film camera – purchased for thousands of pounds at an auction the previous year – to be modified to fit.

Stella only knows such details because Frank has told her. Frank is obsessed with his photography equipment. The day before they caught their flight out here, Stella watched him line up his camera, lenses and film canisters in the rectangle of light coming in through his bedroom window before taking a photograph of them on his phone.

'I'm shooting the tools I use to shoot,' he'd said over his shoulder. 'How meta.'

Stella finishes eating and gathers up the plates to take inside to wash. Something about having Frank around makes her a better daughter, and she can feel it happening. This seems to work the same for Claire too; since she married Frank, she remembers things like how much water Stella's drunk that day.

Stella stacks Frank's plate on top of the rest. He reaches out and puts his hand on her forearm. He's leaning back in his chair with his linen shirt undone, his camera still unzipped from its case. His chest hair is silver, the skin on his bare stomach thick and red-brown.

'Jasmine should lay off you,' he says, 'now Blue's here as distraction.'

Stella thinks of Blue, standing on the edge of the pool in the midday sun. 'Maybe,' she replies.

That evening, all five of them go out for dinner, to a restaurant on the beach.

Stella sits at the head of the table, Jasmine and Blue on either side. Jasmine's wearing a baby-pink sun dress, and has picked out each of her eyelashes with a lot of mascara. Blue isn't wearing any makeup, but her dress is made of gold sequins that throw rainbows across the drinking glasses. Her bare feet are dirty with red dust, and she has a few long, dark hairs growing out of her toes. On her wrists, she's wearing thick silver jewellery that rings when she moves.

'Stop looking at my friend,' says Jasmine. 'It's like, super weird.'

Stella feels the inside of her mouth get dry. She pours herself a glass of water from the bottle and takes a sip.

'Now, now,' says Frank. 'Don't be jealous.'

As the waiter pours Blue's wine, she leans back in her chair and starts speaking to him. Her Spanish is soft and low. The waiter gets his notebook out.

'Hey small fry. You want what the grown-ups are having?'

Stella nods. 'I eat everything. There's nothing I don't eat.'

'My kinda girl.'

There's a huge steel dish of paella with wedges of lemon, a pile of calamari, and a platter of tiny green peppers, scorched black and sprinkled with rocks of salt. Blue teaches Stella how to rip the head from a prawn and suck the brains out of it, and use the shell of one mussel as a pincer to pull the flesh from another. For pudding, there are entire lemons that have been scooped out and filled with ice cream, and a plate of purple figs.

'You know,' says Blue. 'Every fig you eat still contains the corpse of the wasp that pollinated it.'

'For real?' says Stella.

Jasmine hasn't spoken for almost the entire meal, just moved the rice from one side of her plate to the other. Now, she lifts her napkin to her mouth and spits a chewed fig into it. 'That's fucking gross,' she says.

Blue shakes her head. 'It's nature, baby. That prawn you just ate spent most of its life nibbling a bunch of parasites off larger sea creatures to keep them clean. What d'you think of that?'

Jasmine takes a long pull on her wine. 'Just stop talking.'

Claire and Frank laugh. They like Blue, Stella can tell.

'Are you planning to go to university in September?' asks Claire.

Jasmine rolls her eyes, as she does every time Claire speaks. 'She's hoping to go to Sussex, although there's some doubt around whether she'll get the grades.'

'My first choice is Glasgow,' says Blue.

'You and Jasmine'll be living at opposite ends of the country,' says Frank. 'How on earth will you cope?'

'Oh, I'll have a whole new crew by then,' says Blue. 'I won't still be wasting my time with this one.'

Everyone laughs at that, apart from Jasmine. Stella laughs so hard she nearly falls off her chair. When the laughter dies down, Jasmine's looking right at her.

'Oh yeah? Because you've got so many friends yourself.'

'Oi,' says Blue. 'Lay off. I'm her friend.'

'Yeah,' says Stella. '*She's* my friend.'

Jasmine shakes her head. *She's just using you to wind me up.* 'Blue and I have been best friends since we were practically babies.'

'That's what she thinks,' says Blue. 'I'm just in it for the free holidays.'

Claire and Frank laugh more. Stella bites down on the insides of her cheeks.

Blue leans forward, catches Stella's eye, and winks. 'Hey bestie,' she says. 'You wanna split the last fig?'

The next day, Stella wakes late. The sun filters through the wooden shutters. A mosquito, fat with her blood, swims lazily around the top of the net. There's no air con in the house, so Stella spent the night thrashing about in the wet heat, re-angling the fan so that it was pointing at her face.

The door opens, and there's Blue, dressed in a pair of fluorescent orange bikini bottoms and a white crop top, her dark nipples just visible underneath. One of her hands is full of cherries, the other full of stones.

'Morning lazy bones. We're going to the beach.'

'Me and you?'

'Yup, and Jazz.'

Blue swings the door closed behind her. 'Woah. These are so cute.'

She drops the cherry stones in a small pile on the dresser, and reaches down for a pair of trainers that are peeking out from under Stella's bed. She holds them up to the soles of her feet, then tosses them back down again. 'Too small,' she says.

Blue picks up other items of Stella's clothing

from the floor and holds them against herself. 'Can I borrow this?'

Blue pulls the T-shirt over her head. It's green, with little frills at the sleeves. On it is stitched a felt bumble bee and the words *Bee Kind*.

'I only ever wear that as pyjamas.'

'Really? I love it.'

The T-shirt is tight on Blue, but in a good way. It rides up to show a strip of stomach, her belly button as dark and perfect as the cherries she was eating.

By the time they leave the bedroom, Blue's dressed head to toe in Stella's clothes. She's wearing sunglasses decorated at the edges with plastic daisies, and a pair of stretchy shorts so small for her they look like knickers.

Jasmine's waiting on the sofa, swinging a set of moped keys in her fingers. 'What the fuck are you wearing?' she says.

Blue gives a twirl. Stella knows that most grown women in that outfit would look crazy, but Blue manages to pull it off.

'Come on,' says Jasmine. 'We're going.'

'Stella's coming too.'

'Seriously?'

Blue underlines the slogan on her T-shirt with her finger. 'Read it and weep, baby,' she says.

The first time Stella met Jasmine, Frank had just left Jasmine's mother for hers. It was winter, and they went out for breakfast in a new café that had opened near Stella's school. Stella got a hot chocolate with marshmallows that melted and gave a sweet, chemical taste to the milk. Jasmine was wearing foundation so thick her skin looked prosthetic. She looked at her phone under the table the entire time. If Stella closed her eyes, it was almost like Jasmine wasn't there at all.

'Come on Jazzy,' said Frank. 'Say something. Say anything.'

Claire touched him lightly on the arm. 'It's OK, don't push it. She'll talk when she's ready.'

The bill had to be paid at the counter. When they got up to leave, there were lots of people in the queue. Jasmine and Stella went and stood outside. The wind was cold, and Stella pulled her scarf up around her ears.

'Your dad's really nice,' said Stella, through

the material.

Jasmine was standing with her body facing the road, not looking at Stella. 'Well your mum's a fucking homewrecking fucking whore.'

She spoke at an even volume, as if she was saying something completely normal, still looking out over the road as the cars went by. Stella didn't reply. The words stayed in her head like an echo, and she couldn't think of anything else.

When Frank and Claire came outside, they all got in the same car. Jasmine was still living in the house Stella lives in now, and Frank was staying in the flat that Claire and Stella had lived in all Stella's life. Frank gave Jasmine a lift home, and she made him drop her off a block from the house.

'I don't want you setting her off again,' she said, before she climbed out.

Blue swings her leg over the moped, slots the key into the ignition, and slaps the empty part of the seat behind her. 'Hop on,' she says. 'Let's make this pussy roar.'

Blue drives fast. The paths are bumpy and full of sharp turns. Her body feels solid and strong, like hugging a snake. The wind combs Stella's hair. They drive through the pink salt flats, past fields of dry, ploughed earth, pulling over intermittently to let Jasmine catch up. Jasmine's nervous on the moped, whirring along at the speed of the bicycles, looking over her shoulder constantly to check for approaching cars.

It isn't long before they're lost. The beach is small and deserted, with gritty sand. The sea is choppy, mauve jellyfish bobbing like single-use plastic. Blue and Jasmine take their bikini tops off and lean back on the puckered grey rocks to tan.

'You're in my light,' Jasmine says to Stella, though she isn't.

Once the girls become so hot and thirsty that they have to brave the sea, Jasmine devises a game in which Stella has to paddle around her and Blue in circles to make sure they don't get stung.

'Oh please,' says Blue. 'That's practically child labour.'

'I wasn't planning on paying her.'

'It's OK,' says Stella. I don't mind.'

In fact, she doesn't. There's something

heroic-sounding about the set up to her. She'd never been stung by a jellyfish, and doesn't imagine it could hurt that bad. Although Stella sticks to the plan, it's Jasmine that gets stung. Her scream is throaty.

'You've got to piss on it,' says Blue, back on the sand.

Jasmine is hopping on one foot. 'That's disgusting,' she says. Her eyes are wet with tears and a hot-pink rash has flared up on her ankle.

'I swear,' says Blue. 'It neutralises the sting.'

Jasmine frowns, but she lifts her ankle. 'Fine. You do it.'

'Sorry, babe. I went when we were swimming. Small fry might have something to offer.'

Stella sucks her bottom lip.

'Go on then,' says Jasmine.

Stella squats. It takes a while for the piss to come. She's nervous with them both watching over her like that. Her aim isn't particularly good, and she only manages to get a little bit on Jasmine's sting. The rest splashes up around her ankles and across Jasmine's shins. Jasmine squeezes her eyes shut and retches.

'There,' says Blue. 'Wasn't that good bonding?'

Back at the villa, Frank and Claire have left a note on the table saying they've gone into town for dinner, but there's fish from the market in the fridge that the girls can barbeque.

Blue enrols Stella to help. She says she's seen a bunch of samphire down by the lagoon. Stella doesn't know what that is, but she follows. They walk barefoot in silence. Geckos scuttle in the dry-stone walls, and the yellow grass creaks. Blue teaches Stella how to pick the more tender stalks of samphire by snapping them to check the thickness of their stems. They collect them in a sandcastle bucket that Blue found in the garage. When they have enough, they leave the bucket on a low wall and go swimming. The lagoon's warm, and only as deep as Stella's waist. The sun sinks into it as they swim, leaving the sky and the water the same orange-pink.

Back in the shallows, they stand to walk out. The bottom is smooth, slimy clay, and Stella feels her feet sink into it with every step. The swim has shifted Blue's swimming costume, revealing the lighter shade of skin beneath. Water gathers over her body in droplets and runs down her legs. On the thin slip of sand at the shore of the lagoon, Blue carves the words *Stella & Blue 4eva* with a stick.

In the kitchen, they boil the samphire and chop it fine with other ingredients, like capers and red onion, to make a relish. There's a barbeque on the veranda, and Blue lines fillets of white fish over the coals. The floodlights are on in the pool, and the water looks like a huge turquoise crystal.

Jasmine comes out and sits on the veranda, swatting at her ankles to get rid of the mosquitos. She's wearing a beach kaftan made of sheer cotton, and the outline of her bikini can be seen underneath. Her body has wide, soft curves like a Kardashian, whereas Blue is gangly and narrow, with the bones sticking up out in her shoulders. Blue serves the fish, and Stella spoons the relish. Blue and Jasmine drink wine.

Blue talks for a long time about one of the boys she's dating back home, and Stella can't understand half of what she's saying. 'He's a total stoner, but he goes down on me whenever I want.'

After the fish is gone, Stella takes a scoop more relish and eats it plain off the spoon.

'What d'you reckon, small fry?'

'Most delicious thing I've ever tasted. Zingy!'

'Glad you like.'

Stella almost takes another spoonful, but changes her mind. 'Let's save the rest for mum and Frank. I want them to try it.'

Jasmine sniffs. 'They'll be full up on posh shit.'

'Like what?'

'Lobster, probably.'

'A vibe,' says Blue. 'Maybe I should start fucking your dad.'

'Gross,' says Jasmine. 'Please don't.'

Blue licks the length of her knife. 'I'd fuck anyone for a lobster.'

The following day, Frank drives all five of them out to the edge of the island, where the caves have created little swimming pools from the sea. The rocks are sand-coloured and craterous from the spray. Blue and Jasmine swim off to explore the caves, while Frank gets his camera out and waits on the rocks above for the sun to move a fraction. Stella stays below, trying to forget the camera is on her, and watches Claire, who's lying out towels in a sheltered section of the cave for everyone to sit on. She's bought a cool box filled with water bottles and beers, as well as a few bags of salted almonds. The freckles have come out on her face, some of them joining together into age spots. She's wearing a black swimming costume with a green sarong tied around her waist, and the soft skin on the underside of her arms has concertinaed into lots of tiny wrinkles.

The rock edge of the pool is covered in sea urchins, and Frank swims next to Claire as she climbs in, his face close to the water, pointing out the safest spots to step. The sea is teal, and Stella can see a bike wedged in the sand at the bottom.

'What did you guys eat last night?' asks Stella, once they're out.

Frank is wearing expensive sunglasses, and the lenses blink in the sun. 'Lots of things,' he says. 'Tapas.'

'But what? Specifically. Tell me every single thing.'

Claire laughs.

'Alright,' says Frank. 'Um. We had some big fat prawns, Spanish omelette, patatas bravas.'

'Those marinated anchovies that I like. We had lots of those.'

'There was bread and aioli, and some olives.'

'We had an aubergine thing as well. And some delicious little croquettes.'

'So no lobster?'

'Lobster?' says Claire. 'Not that I can think of. Why d'you ask?'

'No reason,' says Stella. 'Just wondering.'

Jasmine and Blue get back a little after that. Jasmine sits down with a beer while Blue climbs up over the rocks. Stella's noticed that Blue is always moving. Even when she sunbathes, she jitters one of her ankles, or ties little plaits into her hair.

'Look,' shouts Blue. 'This is the perfect place to jump.'

Stella isn't so sure. It's high where Blue is standing, and the rock curves outward, so that if Blue didn't push herself off far enough, she could scrape her body on the way down.

'Jazz, get your ass up here. You too, small fry.'

Even getting over to the platform is a little scary, and both Stella and Jasmine have to use their hands to support themselves as they climb. There's just enough space for all three girls to stand side by side on the ledge. The rock bulges beneath them, the sea so far off it looks solid. A cloud passes over the sun, and the water flashes black. It occurs to Stella that Jasmine might push her off, and she shifts slightly towards Blue.

Below, Claire and Frank stand to watch. 'Be careful,' Claire calls.

'On three,' says Blue. 'OK? Three. Two. One.'

It's only Blue that jumps. Jasmine and Stella stay standing. Blue's body is in the air for whole minutes before the sea swallows her whole. Stella watches the white foam spit on the surface and waits.

'Fuck,' says Jasmine.

Blue comes up whooping. 'Come on, pussies,' she shouts.

Jasmine has her arms folded across her chest. 'I'm not doing it'.'

She starts to make her way back down the rock. Stella stands on the platform, contemplating. Underneath her, Blue treads water and waves. The sea sloshes lightly against the rocks. Stella thinks about how if she died when she jumped, it would be all Blue's fault, and their names would be tied together forever.

Stella jumps. The bulge of the rock passes so close to her body she can hear it, like a bus driving too fast down the street. Someone screams, probably her mother. The air feels hard, and the surface of the water even harder. When Stella comes up, she's shaken, certain that her organs have swapped places inside her body. Blue swims to her.

'You good?'

Stella's panting so loud she can barely hear. She grins. 'Yeah,' she says, between pants. 'That was great. That was so, so great.'

Blue puts her thumb in the air so that the others can see. Claire's had her hands over her face, and she takes them down.

'Again?' says Stella, though she doesn't want to.

'You've got balls, small fry. I'm impressed.'

In the car on the way back to the villa, the seats are so hot they burn. Stella puts her head on Blue's shoulder and closes her eyes.

'What shall we eat tonight?' says Frank. 'I can drive via the shop.'

'It's Blue's last night,' says Jasmine. 'We were planning to go out.'

Stella lifts her face to Blue's. 'No. That went way too fast.'

Light comes through the sunroof and shows a faint, dark moustache on Blue's upper lip. Only a few weeks ago, Stella noticed her own in the zoom-in mirror that Frank has in the bathroom, and used his razor to shave it off.

'Come with us,' says Blue. 'You're invited. Isn't she, Jasmine?'

Jasmine doesn't respond, and Frank coughs to fill the silence.

'See,' says Blue. 'I told you she'd be cool with it.'

Frank laughs then, and so does Claire. Stella wonders if Blue was born exceptional, or if it's the kind of thing that happens gradually.

At the villa, Stella sits on the veranda with the adults while Jasmine and Blue shower and get ready to go out. It's almost like before Blue arrived: Claire leafing through a book, Frank loading a new film into his camera. He puts the previous canister carefully into his bag, and lets out a long, low whistle.

'There's some great shots on that sucker,' he says.

Quickly, Stella prays that the best photographs are of her.

'Stell,' says Claire. 'You'll be careful tonight, won't you? Those girls are adults. You don't have to do the things they do.'

'I know, mum.'

A shout comes from inside the house. 'Hey, small fry. Come try this. I think it'll suit you.'

The dress is made of velour in a muted gold colour. Stella puts it on in her bedroom, and Blue tightens the spaghetti straps by tying them in knots on Stella's shoulders. On Blue, the dress would have been shin-length, but on Stella it trails the floor, and she has to lift it every time she takes a step.

'Guapa.'

'What's that?'

'It means gorgeous.'

Stella looks in the mirror.

'Go ahead,' says Blue. 'Play dumb. Act like you don't know.'

'I didn't know! I'd never heard that word before.'

'I mean you're acting like you don't know you're gorgeous.'

Frank drives the girls into town, pulling into a

bus stop to drop them off. He passes Stella a roll of notes through the window, to pay for dinner.

'What about me?' says Jasmine.

'I was getting to you.'

The cobbled streets are strung with fairy lights, and the tiny church is flood-lit. Lots of men run their eyes over Blue as she walks. Stella follows directly behind and pretends it's her that the men are looking at. When they come to the restaurant, Jasmine picks a table that's set up on the street outside. The moon is big and yellow in the gap between the buildings, and Blue orders red wine that comes in a carafe with short, stubby glasses.

'Have a sip,' says Blue.

Stella shakes her head and shivers. 'I've tried wine before. It's horrible.'

'It's not how it tastes, small fry. It's how it makes you *feel*.'

Blue pours her a glass, and Jasmine picks it up and drinks. 'Hey,' says Stella. 'That was for me.'

When Jasmine puts the glass back on the table, it's empty. 'You're twelve years old. Remember?'

'How could I forget.'

Jasmine laughs, for the first time Stella's ever heard. It feels nice.

Blue orders an entire fish that comes on an oval platter, swimming in its own juices. She pops the eyeball out with her fork and places it carefully in the middle of Stella's empty plate.

'That's your dinner. If you're good, you can have the other one after.'

'I know you're joking.'

'I'm deadly serious.'

Stella picks the eyeball off her plate. In her fingers, it feels like the balls of polystyrene that had protected Frank's new lens when it arrived in the post. Stella tosses the eyeball into her mouth and swallows.

No one speaks for a moment. Stella worries she's done the wrong thing. Then Blue slips low into her chair, throws her head back and laughs and laughs. 'I fucking love this kid,' she says.

Stella feels her body float upwards, a little off the seat. Jasmine cuts a fillet away from the fish and places it on Stella's plate. 'Here,' she says. 'To get the taste out. I'll get you some water as well.'

The girls begin to eat. Blue and Jasmine talk about learning to drive, which Jasmine is doing and Blue is avoiding.

'Dad took me out to practice once,' says Jasmine. 'I guess he thought it was a good opportunity for bonding.'

'A good opportunity for mansplaining,' says Blue.

'Literally. The only person he was bonding with was himself.'

'Like that's necessary.'

Jasmine nods. 'He's a shit driver, too.'

'Fuck driving anyway,' says Blue. 'I'd rather get driven.'

'That's probably best for everyone,' pipes up Stella, thinking of her ride on the moped.

Jasmine laughs at that, too.

They're midway through the meal when Blue waves at someone. Stella looks over her shoulder to see a man a few tables away. Jasmine looks too.

'This guy's been eyeing me for ages,' says Blue, not breaking her smile.

The man has hair that looks matted on purpose, and there's a guitar propped against his chair. 'He's fit,' says Jasmine.

'He's alright,' says Blue.

'Yeah,' says Stella. 'Nothing special.'

'What do you know about it, small fry?' says Blue. She calls the man over. 'You fancy buying us a drink?' she says, when he arrives.

'How old is she?' says the man. His accent is maybe French or Italian.

'That's Stella. She's nineteen.'

'And your name?'

'Blue.'

'OK. Now I'm sure you're lying.'

Blue reaches over and pulls the empty chair back from their table. 'We drink vodka,' she says. 'Vodka and orange.'

'What are you doing?' asks Jasmine, once the man is inside the restaurant, standing at the bar.

'What does it look like? You said you fancied him.'

'I said he was fit. It's different.'

'Is it?'

The man comes back with a round tray. He puts the drinks down on the table. Jasmine moves Stella's glass next to hers. This time, Stella doesn't protest. The man sits down. He tells them his name is Nico.

'We have a question for you, Nico,' says Blue.

'Go on.'

'D'you think there's a difference between fancying someone and thinking they're fit?'

Under her makeup, Jasmine goes pink. Nico doesn't notice; he's looking at Blue. 'My English might not be good enough for this question,' he says.

'Just answer. We're having a debate.'

Nico picks up his guitar and starts plucking at the strings. 'What's *fit*?'

'It means hot,' says Blue. 'Sexy, attractive. It's what Jasmine thinks of you.'

Jasmine blushes even more then. She has her eyes on her empty plate, and she looks to Stella like she might start to cry. Nico is smiling a little, amused.

'So, what's your answer?'

'I'd say they're the same.'

Blue grins. 'That means you're with me.'

Nico looks at Blue, and she looks back. The evening is balmy, and their faces are shimmering. Stella thinks that the sounds coming from the guitar are sort of tinny, perhaps out of tune. That look lasts a long time.

The screech of Jasmine's chair against the paving makes Stella jump. She has to run to catch her.

'Are you OK?'

'I'm fine. Leave me alone.'

'That was kinda unfair.'

'What was?'

'You know.'

Jasmine stops. They're at the bottom of the street by now. The fairy lights have run out and things are a shade darker. Jasmine's face is mostly covered by her hair, but Stella can see that her mascara is running.

'I'm used to it,' she says. 'I'm never the first choice.'

Blue arrives then. She's jogged down, and her breathing's loud. 'I've always wanted to do a runner,' she says.

Jasmine wipes the mascara from under her eyes with her index finger. 'Fuck's sake,' she says, turning to make her way back to the restaurant.

At their table, Nico has gone. Perhaps Blue sent him away, or perhaps he was simply afraid of being lumbered with their bill. Stella hopes it is the former. She pulls Frank's money from inside her trainer, and leaves the lot in the middle of the table. Neither Blue nor Jasmine make signs of contributing.

The taxi ride home is taken in silence. Stella rolls the window down, sticks her head out, and watches white stars run through the sky like streamers.

At the villa, Frank and Claire are in bed already, and the girls sit out on the veranda. There's a box of cigarettes on the table, so Jasmine and Blue help themselves to a couple. After Jasmine lights the cigarettes, she uses the matches to light the candles on the table. The girls' faces flicker.

'Isn't it past your bedtime?' says Jasmine.

Blue takes a drag of her cigarette. 'Can you put your insecurity on hold for like, five minutes?'

'Fuck off, Blue.'

'We all know it's not small fry you're pissed off with, or me.'

Jasmine doesn't reply to that. Stella can see the milky way behind her head.

'It's not even Claire,' says Blue. 'It's your arsehole of a dad.'

Jasmine keeps refusing to meet Blue's eye. The ash falls from the end of her cigarette onto the table and scatters.

'He spent ten years of his marriage sleeping with Claire,' says Blue. 'He clean broke your mum's heart. She can't get out of bed for weeks at a time, and he's out here with his new wife and his flash camera. He's an arsehole, Jazz. He's a fucking arsehole. Say it with me.'

'He's an arsehole. He's a fucking arsehole.'

Jasmine stands up and goes into the house. Stella cranes her neck, but the lights are off all through the villa. When Jasmine comes back, Frank's camera bag is slung over her shoulder.

'No,' says Stella.

Jasmine takes the steps down from the veranda. Stella stands up and follows. Blue falls into step behind her. The cool air opens around them, and Stella's eyes adjust as she walks.

'Throw it,' says Blue. 'Let it go.'

Blue's enjoying this, Stella can tell. There's something like laughter in her voice. 'That camera's worth thousands,' says Stella. 'Think of the films. They'll be ruined.'

The splash is big enough to set the sensors

off. The pool lights up to show Frank's bag sinking to the bottom. It quivers gently as it hits the tiles, its strap settling around it like a rosary.

'Fuck,' says Jasmine.

Blue laughs. 'I didn't think you were actually gonna do it.'

'I'll get it,' says Stella. 'I'll get it now. It might be OK.'

'Nah.' Blue lies her hand on Stella's shoulder. 'It's over. That camera's fucked.'

No one says anything for a while. Stella can feel her pulse in the ends of her fingers, all up her neck. A bat sweeps down from the sky, drinks a sip of water from the pool, and flies off into the dark.

'Alright,' says Blue. 'Let's get you kids to bed. That's enough excitement for one night.'

Stella barely sleeps at all. It's just past nine when she hears Frank's voice, slightly raised, through the shutters. 'What the,' he says.

In a short space of time, everyone's out on the veranda. Stella supposed that staying in her room would look guilty, and it seems that Blue and Jasmine thought that too. By this point, Frank is already in the pool.

'What is it?' calls Claire. She looks at Stella, and Stella looks away.

'In the pool,' Frank splutters as he surfaces. Blue chews on her nails.

'My God,' says Claire. 'Is that your camera?'

Frank swims with his bag held above the surface. In her mind, Stella sees the water seeping into all the round outlines of the buttons, the ridges where the Dream Lens has been carved to fit, the film canisters sloshing aqua.

Frank climbs out of the pool and walks back to the veranda. Drops fly off him, and the wet camera slaps at his chest. He passes by Stella, Claire and Blue, until he's standing in front of Jasmine. His face is a strange colour, like something cooked. He leans very close to Jasmine, and she squints back at him. She stands a foot shorter than him, her head angled upwards. It's like that for what feels like hours: nose-to-nose, both shaking, silent but for Frank's ragged breaths. A single tear runs down Jasmine's cheek. The sound of the camera dripping slows to a rhythm.

'It was me,' says Stella. She has the same feeling she had when she ate the fish eye. 'It was me,' she says again.

Jasmine and Blue look at Stella. Jasmine is

crying more now. Frank lowers himself slowly into a chair. The thick skin on his belly makes narrow rolls, and he hangs his head low over them.

'What?' says Claire.

Stella turns and runs through the house. In her bedroom, Blue's velour dress is a loop on the floor. On the dresser, the cherry stones have lost their shine. Stella crawls into bed, pulls her knees up beneath her chin, and waits.

Some hours later, Stella wakes to Blue shaking her gently. 'Small fry. Hey, I'm outta here.'

In the airless garage, Stella climbs into the car. She didn't see Frank on the way through the house, but Claire is sat in the driver's seat, next to Jasmine. Blue's in the back with Stella, her suitcase jammed into the footwell, her legs folded on either side. No one says a word as they drive. The day's so hot the tarmac on the roads is melting. The whole car smells like Blue: coconut oil and Hawaiian Tropic. Stella watches Claire in the wing-mirror. It's clear from her eyes that she's been crying.

The drive to the port takes fifteen minutes. When they arrive, Claire waits with the car while Stella and Jasmine walk Blue to the ferry. The boat is huge and white, chugging black smoke into the cobalt sky. The girls stand on the concrete jetty to say their goodbyes, their shadows long and thin in the afternoon sun.

'You're pretty badass, small fry, you know that?'

Stella shoves her hands deep into the pockets of her shorts. 'Thanks.'

Behind Blue, the edges of the jetty ripple in the heat. There's a slope set up for boarding, and a man checking tickets. He waves Blue over. The boat's scheduled to leave any minute. It'll take Blue to the mainland, where she'll catch her flight back to London.

'Well,' says Blue. 'It's been real.'

She pulls Jasmine and Stella into a hug, and they stand like that for a while, sticky against each other. Stella can feel her heartbeat pressed up to Blue's body.

Jasmine and Stella stay a little too far apart after Blue walks away, leaving space for her to change her mind. Instead, the ramp lifts and the boat starts to pull out of the port. After a minute or so, Blue appears on the flat roof of the ferry and stands with her hands on the railings, a black silhouette against the wide sky. Stella waves and waves as Blue gets smaller. When the ferry is unintelligible from the other boats in the distance, Stella and Jasmine turn back to the car park.

'Hey. Thanks, by the way.'

Stella slows, uses her hand to shield her face, looks at Jasmine, and nods.

Through the car windscreen, Stella can see her mother fanning herself with a map of the island. 'Shotgun,' says Stella.

Jasmine doesn't fight her, only gets into the back seat without a word. Stella stands for a moment in the heat, looking out at the horizon, before cracking open the passenger door and climbing in herself.

About the Authors

Kerry Andrew is a composer, performer and author and the winner of four British Composer Awards. Kerry's debut novel, *Swansong,* was published by Jonathan Cape in 2018, and a second novel, *Skin,* was published in 2021.

Jenn Ashworth's first novel, *A Kind of Intimacy,* was published in 2009 and won a Betty Trask Award. On the publication of her second, *Cold Light* (Sceptre, 2011), she was featured on the BBC's The Culture Show as one of the UK's twelve best new writers.

Anna Bailey was born in 1995 and grew up in Gloucestershire, studying Creative Writing at Bath Spa University, before moving to Texas and later Colorado. Their first novel is the literary thriller *Tall Bones* (2021).

Vanessa Onwuemezi is a writer and poet living in London. She is the winner of *The White Review* Short Story Prize 2019 and her work has appeared in literary and art magazines, including *Granta, frieze* and *Prototype*. Her debut short story collection, *Dark Neighbourhood,* was published by Fitzcarraldo Editions, in 2021 and was named one of *The Guardian*'s best books of 2021. It was shortlisted for the Republic of Consciousness Prize 2022.

Saba Sams has been published in the *Stinging Fly, Granta* and *Five Dials,* among others. She was shortlisted for *The White Review* Short Story Prize in 2019. Her debut collection of short stories, *Send Nudes,* was published in 2022 and has been longlisted for the Edge Hill Prize 2022. She studied Creative Writing as an undergraduate at The University of Manchester,.